DEAD FALSE

DEAD FALSE

A Murder Mystery

M.R. Carroll

THE MERCURY PRESS

The publisher gratefully acknowledges the financial assistance of the Canada Council and the Ontario Arts Council.

Cover design by Gordon Robertson
Edited by Beverley Daurio
Composition and page design by TASK

Printed and bound in Canada by Metropole Litho
Printed on acid-free paper
First Edition
1 2 3 4 5   02 01 00 99 98

Canadian Cataloguing in Publication Data

Carroll, M.R. (Michael R.)
Dead false
ISBN 1-55128-066-3
I. Title. II. Series
PS8555.A7714D42 1998   C813'.54   C98-932203-3
PR9199.3.C37D42 1998

Represented in Canada by the Literary Press Group
Distributed in Canada by General Distribution Services

THE MERCURY PRESS Toronto, Canada M6P 2A7

*To three women, two lost and one found:
my grandmother, who first told me stories;
my mother, whose own story was cut short;
and Carol Ann, who inspires me to write more stories.*

Bear in mind that when a man seeks the
impossible, it is only just that the possible
be denied him.
— Miguel de Cervantes, *Don Quixote*

STATION I

"Hello, may I please speak to Carole Rutland?"

A voice on the phone. An old woman's voice. A mother's voice, maybe. Or an old lady working for some collection agency. Carole was like that: hunted by bailiffs and bill collectors, always looking over her shoulder, watching for demons, the real and the imaginary.

I don't know why I thought the voice might belong to Carole's mother. Surely a mother knows where her daughter is. The voice sounded puzzled and hopeful, even apologetic, and some old lady bill collector wouldn't sound like that, would she?

"Carole?" I answered, pretty puzzled myself. "I used to share a house with her, but that was over a year ago."

"Do you know where I could reach her?" the old woman's voice quavered.

"No, I—" But I didn't get it all out. The line went dead.

Standing there holding the receiver, I cursed myself for not finding out who the caller was. Then I wondered how my number had gotten connected with Carole. In the house we'd shared we'd all had separate phones, but Carole had lost hers— unpaid bills again— and had probably given out my number instead, a number I still had despite moving. But that had been a year and a half ago. Why a phone call now? Surely a mother knows where her daughter is.

I let things prey on my mind. I've always been that way. That time in that house with Carole and a lot of other losers had been a champion time for me to let things prey on my mind. In a sense, I'd been hiding out. Holed up in a sewer with a lot of scared, broken people. A loser on the lam going nowhere.

But I was healthier now, I told myself. That time was past and I was on my feet again, even if I was still an unemployed journalist. At least I didn't brood so much. The break-up with Laura was long ago, so I thought, standing there like an idiot with the receiver in my sweaty hand.

Carole Rutland— what did she mean to me? A looney. A real nutcase.

Straitjacket material. Good-looking. Yeah, damn good-looking. But spaced out. Gone to the moon and still running. Scared shitless. Of what? Of everything, yet proud and arrogant, as if she were a queen, or a lost princess of forgotten nobility. Couldn't hold a job down for ten seconds, up to her ears in debt, evicted more times than she had years, but as haughty and contemptuous as Bette Davis in *Jezebel,* or Vivien Leigh in you know what.

We used to sit in my room and talk over coffee and cookies. That's what we used to eat and drink when we were on friendly terms— my coffee, her cookies. She told me once that her family originally came from South Africa. Afrikaners. One of her ancestors was a general. Name got changed in Canada, but back in South Africa it had been de Ruitland.

I still remember the many times she told me that. Her back would get really straight. She'd flick her ash-blonde hair away from her face and stare at me with those bright green off-centre eyes. "De Ruitland," she'd whisper, as if it were a mantra, "General André Cornelius Jacob de Ruitland." You'd think she was related to the queen of England. And then those green eyes would catch the cover of one of my books on witchcraft. I am still fascinated with things occult, from a purely historical-cultural-folkloric perspective, of course; no Bermuda Triangles, hollow earths, or Edgar Cayces for me, thank you. She'd run one long pale finger over a book's spine and say, "They know not what they do," or just, "Witches," and then she'd chuckle to herself, mumbling, "One has to be careful, very careful, about certain things."

Carole fancied herself as something of a witch. In her room, directly across from mine in that ramshackle house, she'd burn incense, chant for hours on end, and fill page after page with incredible gibberish. Poetry, she called it. When she wasn't doing that, she'd fill up vast sheets of butcher paper à la Emily Carr with talentless watercolour and tempera fantasies, usually with a galactic theme.

Carole thought of herself as an artist as well as a witch. What kind of artist depended on her mood. One day she'd be into what she called Martian Poetry. The next day it'd be orgonic-post-Reichian aura painting. After reading about Isadora Duncan, Carole was a misunderstood dancer. Other times she'd be in a lather to write a play about her invisible friends from the twenty-third dimension. Not too long before she moved out— was kicked out— she'd been all set to write the kiddy book of the century, another Alice or Oz, no doubt, which would be zapped to the unwary reader from Tau Ceti.

I was too pragmatic, perhaps, even in my chronic romanticism, to ever figure Carole out. She lived life as if she were perpetually in hiding. She'd probably been that way since childhood. In one of her lucid moments she told me she'd graduated from Queen's University with a bachelor of science in biology and that she'd worked in a lab as a technician for a month or two until she couldn't take the "bullshit," as she put it, any more. "What bullshit?" I asked once, but all I got in response was, "You know," and a strange nod.

Carole had also been a model at one time. Showed me her portfolio once. It consisted of glossy eight-by-tens of Carole with a lot of make-up and a toothy smile; she was good-looking without the make-up. When I asked her why she'd quit modelling, she got glassy-eyed and stared out at the park our house was next to— we were sitting on the tumbledown porch at the time. She stared fixedly at a big maple as if it would get away from her if she didn't nail it down with those shiny green eyes. She stared and said, "Them." Well, of course, I asked who "them" might be, being literal-minded, but Carole kept staring at the tree and sort of told me, or the sky at large, that the trees, the birds, the very sky itself, were more than just trees, birds, sky— they were, they really *were*. And then she drilled me with those fevered eyes, now red-rimmed with whatever inner anguish tormented her, and asked me, "Do you understand? Do you see?" But before I could say anything, not that I really knew what to say, she got up, closed her portfolio with a loud snap, and said, as she made her way back into the house, "Too much make-up? You're just like them."

Paranoia? Schizophrenia? I'm not a psychiatrist. Who knows? Years ago, in university, I took a class on James Joyce in which the subject of schizophrenia came up, as perhaps it invariably does with Joyce. We were talking about split personalities, and one of the students, suddenly a bit bug-eyed, sharply upbraided us for confusing split personality with schizo-phrenia. All year this student had scarcely uttered a peep. For the rest of the seminar, as we carefully avoided mentioning schizophrenia, he glowered and grumbled. The students on either side of him shifted their chairs as far from him as they could get. Strangely, we never saw the guy again.

But back to Carole. That night, after our "conversation" on the porch, she chanted rather than slept. I'd sleep for an hour or two, wake up, hear her chanting, "They're coming, coming, yes, they're coming," then I'd fall back asleep, a little embarrassed, a little angry, a lot confused. Somewhere in the middle of the night I woke to hear her say, "I could have used the knife." That was like a bathtub of cold water dumped on my head. I sat bolt upright on my futon, got up, went to the door, and listened. "Just wait," she was saying in a very loud whisper. "Just wait. My friends are coming, and there's always the knife." I knew all this was directed at me. I'd joined the long list of Carole's enemies, the seen and unseen.

The next day Carole stopped me on our landing and planted two homemade cookies in my hand. "A peace offering," she said, and we were friends again. After a fashion.

In the weeks that followed, Carole would leave lit cigarettes every-where— on window sills, on the bathroom sink, on the arm of a chair in the communal living room, even once on the big red fire alarm in the hallway. Frequently I'd hear running water in the bathroom and think Carole was taking a bath. Then I'd spot water flowing out into the hallway and I'd open the door to find nobody in the can and a tub of scalding water sending off steam as it gushed onto the cracked linoleum like a thermal Niagara Falls.

Things went downhill for Carole and me after that. One day, when I came home from a night of listless drinking, I smelled something burning in the downstairs kitchen. It turned out to be a pot of what had been rice. The water had long since boiled off, and the black crud in the pot was sending off a billowy stink.

After I shut off the gas, I noticed the pot was mine. Someone had almost burned a hole in it— quite the feat! Then my foot bumped something under the antique cast-iron stove. Bending down, I discovered a cache of pots and pans— my pots and pans— all of them encrusted with mouldy food. Just then, Carole sashayed into the kitchen.

"Oh, it's you," she said, frowning slightly.

"Yeah, it's me. Is this yours?" I demanded, pointing at the destroyed pot.

"My rice! What did you do to it?"

"What did I do to it? Christ, are you crazy?"

Carole's face blanched. "Crazy?" she croaked. Then, before I knew it, she grabbed my head with both hands and smacked it against a cupboard, as if it were a basketball and she were Michael Jordan.

The back of my skull just missed the corner of the cupboard. Instinctively I raised my fist, all set to drive her into the next century, but the expression on her face stopped me. She stood there expectantly, as if she wanted me to hammer her. The look on her white face, part defiant, part ecstatic, part knowing, scared me more than her sudden assault.

I beat it out of the kitchen, mumbling something about "crazy idiots." Before I got to the stairs, though, I heard her say, "I am not fucking crazy! I am not fucking crazy! I am not fucking crazy!" She kept that up for quite some time. Oddly enough, her bouncing my head off the cupboard was the most intimate thing we ever shared. Not long after that she was evicted.

We had four other roommates, and one in particular, Herbert Sutcliffe, a sometime cabbie from Yorkshire, inflamed Carole's already flammable personality with pyromaniacal glee. Two crazies in one house already chockablock with humanity's leftovers does not a peaceful home make. Herbert's typical morning greeting to Carole was usually, "Hullo, slut, how's business?" Carole's reactions ranged from frosty evil eye through ever-louder door slamming, to outright hysterics.

Carole might have been nuts, but Herbert gave me the creeps. He was given to sayings like, "Cats, something about the feline in them..." And all the while he'd be sharpening his favourite butcher knife. The cat in question was the household stray— a ragged, one-eyed tabby which, not unlike Carole, would curl its back and squint a fat green orb at Herbert whenever Herbert got too close.

Herbert drove a cab, but he was always getting parking and speeding tickets. I suspected he doubled as a pimp or something. His usual hack stand was near the sleazy hotels close to Allan Gardens. Once, when we ran into each other on the stairs, Herbert buttonholed me and told me out of the blue that he'd been a guest of the Queen Street Mental Health Centre. When I told Carole that, her eyes got bigger. She had been pretty certain he was a would-be rapist; after that, she was certain. She maintained that Herbert, whenever he clumped downstairs from his attic room, would linger on our landing, standing outside her door, listening, waiting, breathing. Of course, Carole believed in Golems, so who knows?

Added to this merry crew were a couple of male beach bunnies on the lam from 1960s Vancouver. They'd been too young for the hippie scene in that decade, but they'd made up for it in later decades. Brent Stone was a lanky blond who wore Adidas, chinos, and a sailing sweatshirt regardless of the season. Usually stoned, no pun intended, addicted to his Walkman, supposedly a photographer, obsessed with sailing, and a proud owner of the complete works of rocker Steve Miller, Brent had a Harlequin romance name wedded to a Haight-Ashbury Beach Boy cum Bowery Boy personality.

The flip side of the West Coast dynamic duo was Iggy Klein. Iggy's diminutive size— he wasn't much over five feet— was made up for by his impressively long, flowing black hair, which he parted in the middle of his pointy head. Add granny glasses, a big nose, an easy grin, and... I'm not sure what you have.

Iggy— his real name was Igor, seriously— was an itinerant carpenter. He specialized in stairways to nowhere, and people even bought them occasionally. Like pet rocks, canned fresh air from New Mexico, crystal pyramids, and pink flamingoes, stairways to nowhere, Iggy fervently believed, might really take off someday. This North Vancouver gnome's other occupation was collecting records. He must have had ten thousand; it seemed as if he had every rock LP ever pressed. Thanks to creditors and lagging sales on stairs to nowhere, though, Iggy didn't have a stereo, let alone a CD player, a technological marvel the Ig didn't believe in.

Brent and Iggy, our two adorable love children, were courtesy of our landlord, Warren Crane. He'd known them in the old days when he'd been a drug dealer on Granville in Vancouver. All three of them had obviously thought Toronto would provide greener pastures, although Brent constantly pined for the sea, grudgingly making do with the woefully inadequate surge of Lake Ontario.

And then there was Pavel, a Czech gambler in exile. None of us knew much about Pavel, though we all imagined he had some unhealthy connection with the Russian Mafia, ex-KGB torturers, or both. Pavel rarely emerged from his room except to journey to the track or go to the can. Bill collectors, bailiffs, loan sharks, ex-wives— no one could raise Pavel from his room when he was incommunicado. Even our landlord, a master at evasion himself, generally failed to pry Pavel out of his lair come rent day. On those rare and fleeting occasions when Pavel was flush, meaning a win at the track, he would fry up a bushel of onions, throw in a little Prague ham, and wash it all down with Pilsner Urquell. When it came to beer, he had expensive tastes and a longing for the old country. The beer was the only thing on which we saw eye to eye.

The peripheral characters changed, but this was the regular crew infesting that house on the park when Carole lived there. Hearing Carole Rutland's name on the telephone brought it all back— the mice, the cockroaches, the lunatics, the dry rot, the brawls, the sickly sweet smell of not-so-good pot, the delirium, the drinking, the cold, dank, slimy feel of bottom-of-the-basement sludge. Things were better now; at least I had different digs, and occasionally I got work editing computer manuals or writing articles on the virtues of saving string. And relative affluence, or is it effluent, breeds nostalgia, and maybe a little superior concern. You know, "There but for the grace of God go I."

I was pretty certain that Carole was still out there in the chill night-time, still running in the half-world of evictions, dead-end jobs, welfare, and locked-room delirium tremens. I knew that world, still dreamed it nearly every night. I was high and dry now, most of me, out of the slime on the slaughterhouse floor of all our expectations. I could throw a lifesaver to someone. I could lead the way out of that pit of urban lizards and vermin. Space Age Orpheus. Dime-store Galahad. James Michael Finnegan, aka Mickey Finnegan, hero of our time. I decided to go look for her.

Why bother with a looney like that? Remember the knife? Beware of crazies bearing chocolate chip cookies? The truth was that I had nothing better to do: time on my hands and unemployment cheques in the mail. What's more, Carole was a dish, and someone had once told me— Jerry Bauch, I think— that crazies were hot stuff in bed. Besides, maybe I'd get a story out of it.

STATION II

It's not easy to find somebody if they really want to go missing, especially if the person looking is an amateur. I tried the phone company, but knew the answer before I even called information. Lots of Rutlands in the phone book— I tried them all— but none of them proved to be Carole's mother, let alone Carole herself. Carole had gone to Queen's, so I tried Kingston. Maybe her mother lived there. No dice. Then I realized I was assuming Carole's mother's surname was Rutland. Who knows? Maybe Carole's mother had remarried or something. Maybe she'd reverted to her maiden name. Maybe she'd left the city. I suppose I could have gone on wasting time with telephone operators and such, but I had a better idea.

I decided to try the University of Toronto. Carole had raved about a creative writing course she'd taken there, no doubt as an adjunct to her exploration of extraterrestrial poetry. I knew a professor at University College and thought he might be able to help me get Carole's permanent address or her mother's whereabouts. Funny word, *permanent,* in conjunction with Carole. With some luck, I could trace Carole's current refuge. If nothing else, maybe I'd find out if the voice on the phone had really been Carole's mother, or just a sneaky bill collector.

University College was everything a university building should be— neo-Romanesque, lots of ivy, a little church-like. Inside the massive pile it was gloomy and damp, the way I remembered Cambridge and Oxford being. Maybe somewhere in the bowels of the university there was a department devoted to ensuring the campus maintained the correct atmosphere, at least in the older buildings. The dampness conjured up tweed, tutorials over tea, thesis dissertations on turd imagery in *Tamburlaine,* and quaffing bitters in a tavern Christopher Marlowe might once have frequented. The U of T liked to think of itself in the same breath as England's medieval monuments to higher education. In the fall, classes not quite a month old, squirrels chasing one another through musty piles of leaves, a tang of winter in the air already though still warm, the illusion worked, for the moment.

Once inside the college I got disoriented as usual. Academia does that to me, especially old academia. All that dark, aged wood, mildew, and funny furniture-polish smell, I guess. Wending my way through stained-glass passageways and over wooden parquet floors, I nearly collided with a burly man in a beige car coat. He had just come out of an office marked Garrett Macpherson. He didn't look Scottish, nor did he look professorial. He looked like a cop, and maybe Polish. He stared at me hard, as if I were a suspect, his big face glowering, and ploughed on down the corridor. I had an impression of broken nose, jug ears, high cheekbones, crew cut, and beady eyes. I watched him, ratty brown fedora in hand, head for the main lobby, where he met two colleagues in uniform. Cops on campus. Unusual.

I finally found Jack Malone's office, a tiny book-fortified cubbyhole stuck away in a particularly moist cranny of the college; I'd been there once or twice in the long-ago past. He had a window, though, and it was open, as was his door. Malone was standing at the window as I strode in.

"This place looks like a used bookstore. Setting up shop, Jack?"

He spun around and grinned at me. I'd taken a course on Romantic poetry from him years ago at another university, but he hadn't changed a whit. He was still wearing the same coffee-stained green corduroy jacket he'd always worn, with the incongruous paisley cravat, beige, almost yellow, work dungarees, and construction boots. His wild black hair, which always looked as if he'd been given an electric shock, was a little greyer— although that might have been chalk dust— but the grin was as sprawling, the blue eyes as merrily explosive, and the stubby-fingered hand shot out as hard and fast as I remembered. Jack's handshake was like wind in steel; it was over before you knew it, but its strength lingered. Jack did everything fast. As a poet, English teacher, dedicated spelunker, television and radio commentator, better-than-average tennis player, and gourmet cook, time was something he never had enough of. That's probably why he never combed his hair.

"Well, well," he said, sticking a finger in his ear and digging away. "It's been a long time, Mickey."

"Yeah, I guess it has been."

"How's Laura?"

I stared out the window. Hundreds of yellow-helmeted engineering students were holding a rally on the front campus. Whatever gathering illusions of imagined Cambridge gentility I might have been harbouring were chased out of my head by the thundering shouts of the novice engineers, who were standing around an open-pit fire. I wasn't sure if they were roasting the sacrificial bull or engaging in some mass al fresco engineering problem.

"Pagan ritual," Jack suggested. He, too, was staring out the window.

"Just what I was thinking."

"Was it?"

I looked at him. "How long has it been since we last saw each other?"

"Two years, maybe more."

"I got your book, but I guess that was a while ago, too."

"*White on White*. I figured you must have loved it. Too overcome with emotion to tell me."

"Still writing poems about looney bins?"

"I'm writing short stories these days. Got a new book coming out. Little press called Muskrat, or is it Musk-ox? I'm even working myself up for a novel."

"How's Brigit?"

"You didn't answer *my* question."

"Laura? I thought you knew... we broke up."

"When?"

"About two years ago."

The engineers were tossing something on a blanket. Probably an unfortunate arts student who'd strayed off the path and into the wrong forest. They were enjoying themselves; the noise was deafening.

"Let's sit," Jack said, closing the window. "Enough anthropology for one day."

I swept a dog-eared volume of Byron's *Don Juan* and a bundle of seminar papers off a sagging overstuffed chair and sat down. Jack slid behind his desk which, heaped with odds and ends, looked like a table in a rummage shop.

"Coffee?" he asked.

"Sure."

"Give me a moment. The java's around the corner in the English office. Sugar and cream, right?"

"I bet you still know the grade I got on the course I took with you."

"B-. How could I forget? My late-blooming anti-prodigy."

He got up and hurried out of the office. While he was gone, I looked around. On one wall hung a framed print of Géricault's *Raft of the Medusa*. A trio of West African masks shrieked silently in one corner near the window and behind the desk. Malone, in his youth, had worked in some indeterminate capacity in Nigeria. He'd also been a cultural attaché at the American embassy in Stockholm. In still another life he'd had something to do with an oil company, Gulf or Shell, in Indonesia. The guy got around. Half buried in the clutter of the desk was a photo of Jack's wife, Brigit. Blonde, of course, but spun-gold blonde, not light brown trying to be blonde like Laura, or tawny blonde like Carole. Brigit looked like an actress, every guy's dream of an actress— retroussé nose, a teasing, dangerous smile that was inviting at the same time, dancing emerald eyes that even in the photograph burned a hole in your head, and all that long blonde stuff that swept around her perfect face and stopped short of her Ingrid Bergman shoulders.

"She's just about finished her M.A. in psychology," Jack said, dangling a styrofoam cup of coffee in my face.

I looked up at him and took the coffee. "Thanks," I mumbled.

Jack sat down at his desk again. "What can I do for you? I have a feeling this isn't just a social call, and I've got a class in half an hour."

"What's with the cops? I bumped into a hefty specimen on my way in here."

Jack's grin nearly splashed off his jaw as it turned into a sneer, his peaked eyebrows arching into exclamation points. "Ah, you noticed. Haven't you been reading the papers in your hideout?"

"Papers?"

"Christ, Mickey, just what have you been doing with yourself?"

"I've been reading Proust."

"Really? I thought Hemingway and hard-boiled were more to your taste."

"And Byron."

He laughed at that. "Want to mark some seminar papers for me?"

"What about the fuzz?"

"You're not keeping up on your slang, Mickey."

I frowned. "Why the cops, Jack? The university has its own police force, doesn't it?"

"Not when it comes to big stuff."

"Big stuff? Here?"

"Even murder most foul happens under the ivy. Hell, back in the 1850s when the first University College was built, there were two stone carvers, a Russian named Ivan Reznikoff and another guy called Paul Diabolos, maybe a Greek. Anyway, Diabolos really had a hate on for Reznikoff. He even carved a demonic caricature of him on the western end of the south wing. It's still there, in the part of the building that a later fire didn't gut. Well, ol' Rezzy didn't take kindly to Diabolos's artwork. Seems they had the hots for the same girl, who remains nameless. The lady, of course, was a real sore point between our boys, and one night Rezzy hid out and waited for Diabolos to keep a fake appointment with the girl that Rezzy had craftily engineered. When Diabolos showed up, Rezzy lunged at him with an axe. But the blade missed and got stuck in a door. Diabolos didn't hang around for the replay. He took a powder up the tower stairs, and Rezzy chased after him. When they got to the top, Diabolos pulled a dagger and stabbed Reznikoff, then tossed his body down to the bottom of the tower.

"They never did find Rezzy. No one knew what happened to Diabolos or the girl, and it was assumed Rezzy moved on to some other stone-carver job. For decades students and profs reported strange goings-on and odd bumps in the night, and the ghost of University College was born. Nobody knew about poor Rezzy, though, until a fire destroyed most of the college in the 1890s. In the rubble of the tower, they found all that was left of Ivan Reznikoff— a skull, some bones, and a silver buckle."

"Charming story, Jack. You just make it up?"

"Would I lie to you, Mickey? It's all true, I swear. I thought you'd like it. I've always been rather intrigued by Mr. Diabolos and his anonymous love. I imagine her as a blonde."

"I bet you do. So is this your coy way of telling me that someone's been murdered on the campus?"

"Hell, no. Nothing as exciting as that. Just a little thievery. Our beloved university has lost something valuable, and the good gentlemen from the police are trying to help us find it. Actually, the ex-wrestler you collided with was in here earlier today, questioning me."

"I didn't think you spent much time in your office. You never used to."

"Fall cleaning. In with the new and in with the old. I'm redistributing the wreckage. Anyway, we've lost a priceless manuscript."

"You keep saying *lost*. Where's the thievery?"

"Okay, *stolen*. A Shakespeare manuscript, to be exact."

"I thought there weren't any manuscripts."

"There is now, or was. What's more, it's a lost play. Found, now lost again. It's called *Cardenio,* and this place has been buzzing since it went missing a few days ago."

"What's this university doing with a lost play of Shakespeare?"

"You do this hallowed pile an injustice. Actually, Macpherson is the man to talk to. He's the one who found it. English Lit.'s Man of the Hour, you might say. 'Fame sometimes hath created something of nothing.'"

"Shakespeare?"

"No, Thomas Fuller, seventeenth-century scholar and biographer."

"I thought you were a Romantic."

"So sue me."

"Is this Shakespeare manuscript in his own handwriting? Is it authentic?"

"How should I know? Shakespeare's not my field."

"But you always have an opinion."

Jack sipped his coffee and chuckled. "Not this time. No one got a chance to see it, except Macpherson, and Brownlee, the head of the department. But enough of phantom Shakespeare. You aren't doing an article on crime on campus, are you?"

"I'm not doing an article on anything. I... well, it's hard to explain."

"Shoot."

"I'm trying to find out where a woman named Carole Rutland is living."

"I didn't know the missing persons bureau was located in my office."

"She was a student here. Took a creative writing course a while back."

"I teach a creative writing course. What did you say her name was?"

"Carole Rutland."

He got up and went over to a cardboard filing cabinet. When he pulled on one of the drawers, the whole thing nearly collapsed. "Rutland, Rutland, Rutland," he mumbled as he thumbed through the files. "Ah, here we are."

"She took the course before I knew her, probably two years ago or so, but you might be able to get her parents' address over in student records."

"You think we professors can waltz over there and have our way with their computers?"

"Maybe not their computers..."

"No need, anyway. I've got an address of a friend of hers here. She might be able to help you."

"How come you've got an address of one of her friends?"

"Creative writing students are special."

"Are they?"

"Especially tall blonde ones."

"You remember her?"

"Sort of. Wild eyes, wrote like she looked. I've still got some of her poetry. Here, take a look."

He handed me a sheet of black paper with a poem written in white ink. When I looked up at him, he said, "She told me she liked black paper. Something about it *being* her poem." I glanced at the hastily scrawled words:

In

there

in me

my friend

hot and hard

talking

feeling

an asteroid

out there

but in

in me

my wetness

probing

pushing

warming me

as it fucks

me

up there

so close

"Interesting," I said, handing it back to him.

"Penis poems. All the girls who take my class write them. I'm sure there's a thesis in it somewhere. A lot of them grow up and write this kind of stuff for a living. Some of them even teach here."

"Do they usually have stuff about asteroids and outer space?"

"No, now that you mention it. Carole was hung up on the starry firmament."

"You seem to remember a whole lot about her."

"I try to get to know my students."

"Like Brigit?"

"Only one I've married so far. I even act as matchmaker. You and Laura, for example."

"You said something about a class, didn't you?" I said, getting to my feet. "Maybe I should get that address from you."

"Why do you want to find Carole Rutland, Mickey?"

"Curiosity. I used to share a house with her. Sort of interested in what happened to her."

"Is that all?"

"Yeah, that's all."

He looked at me wonderingly, wrote the address on a slip of paper, and handed it to me. "I don't know what good it'll do you, but if you can find the friend, maybe she'll know how to reach Carole."

I glanced at the address: Sharon Praeger, 3 Lenore Avenue, Ward's Island, Toronto. Tel: 555-1953.

"The island people are pretty permanent in a temporary sort of way. She might be there still."

"Why this address? I mean, how come you've got it?"

"You already asked me that."

"You didn't answer."

"It's the only address, or phone number, Carole ever gave me. And I'd wager it's the only one the university's got, too. Maybe she was staying with this Sharon Praeger, or maybe she just doesn't like giving out her real address. A woman of mystery. Goes with the intergalactic image."

"Yeah, I suppose so. Well, thanks, Jack."

"Oh, before you go, Mickey, now that you've resurfaced, why don't you drop by our house? I know Brigit would like to see you. Actually, we're having a party— launching of my book of short stories and all that. Lot of faculty types will be there, even a few writers. Lots of booze and eats. Social event of the season. What about it?"

"Sure," I said. "I'd like to see Brigit."

"And Conor," he added.

"Right. Your new son. I guess not so new now. I thought you were going to call this one Percy."

"Bysshe, actually, but I'm not that cruel." He grinned the way I remembered him doing when he was about to skewer an unsuspecting undergraduate who'd had the temerity to correct one of his rare mistakes. "So it's settled. You know my address. Tomorrow night, around nine. Okay?"

"Okay."

I thanked him again and made my way out of the gloom, damp, and ivy into the waning sunshine of a day grown colder. The engineers were still out on the grass. Somehow they'd gotten some beer, and things were really getting lively. Gone totally were images of punting on the Cam or *Brideshead-Revisited*-like thoughts of Oxford. The scene was now more reminiscent of a crowd getting out of an English football match.

Sticking up to the south was the concrete shaft of the CN Tower, its red aircraft warning lights blinking rapidly. It was curious how you could see the Tower no matter where you were in the city. It always seemed to be watching from afar.

Off to one side of the stone steps leading up to the college was the big cop in the beige car coat. He was wearing the brown wool fedora, which looked as if he stuffed it in his pocket with great regularity. The cop seemed to be watching the engineers cavort, but I could have sworn he was staring at me. Turning away from him, I shivered and tried to find some warmth in my jacket.

I thought about checking out Paul Diabolos's monstrous portrait of his rival, Reznikoff, but nixed the idea. The engineers might be looking for something else to roast, and they'd love me.

STATION III

It was drizzling when I took the ferry to Ward's Island the next morning. I'd told Sharon Praeger on the phone that I was a journalist and was interested in talking to her. I could have asked her about Carole over the phone, but I thought the best policy was to talk to her in person. That way, at least, she couldn't hang up on me.

Just telling her I was a journalist seemed to be enough. The island people were a beleaguered bunch. For decades the Metro government had tried to seize the islanders' houses so it could turn the land, which it owned, into a park. Not so long ago, with the City of Toronto and the province on their side, the islanders had successfully staved off the ogreish Metro Council and were allowed to stay put. But now a new element had been introduced. No one on the two residential islands— Algonquin and Ward's— trusted the recently created megacity of Toronto. Who knew what future tricks it might be dreaming up? I allowed Sharon Praeger to think I was doing a piece on the situation. The islanders cherished every bit of positive PR they could get, even if the war seemed finally over.

I'd been to Centre Island, mainly an amusement park, a few times, but never to Ward's. The lake was an icy gun-metal green, swarms of sea gulls screeched overhead and swooped in the slate-grey sky, and on the horizon lay the islands, so flat that the semi-nude trees growing on them seemed to sprout from the water without benefit of soil.

Most of the passengers on the ferry appeared to be island people. Women in green and blue slickers, khaki pants, and heavy canary corduroy trousers and white running shoes stood surrounded by well-fed, undoubtedly well-educated little boys and girls who strained against the railings as the ferry ploughed landward. Men in either plaid lumber jackets, hooded sweat suits or bulky off-white Shetlands— all with stiff, new unfaded blue jeans— talked in groups or stared singly into the churning water. Many carried large packages and bundles— Saturday shopping, no doubt. A few had building supplies and equipment in little carts. Somehow the whole bunch reminded me of people I'd encountered on the British Columbia ferries that serviced coastal islands such as Saltspring, Hornby, and Gabriola. Except these men didn't sport ponytails and granny glasses; nor did the women wear sandals and peasant dresses. The Toronto island people were youngish urban professionals by way of crunchy granola. At least this bunch was.

When the ferry docked, I set out for Sharon Praeger's house. The little streets that made up the Ward's Island community were actually sidewalks lined with cottages in various stages of construction. The cottages could have been plucked right out of the Muskoka bush to the north and plunked down here. Woodsmoke permeated the air and the sounds of saws and hammers were everywhere. The islanders had always been busy building, patching, and improving, even when such renovations were illegal.

It didn't take me long to find the house on Lenore Avenue, a little clapboard affair painted chartreuse. Its neighbours on either side were unfinished black tarpaper things with a lot of pine framework exposed. Praeger's house, by contrast, was neat and well maintained. It even had a glass bubble on the roof— solar energy. I was willing to bet Sharon once donated money to the Sandinistas, protested against the killing of whales, cried every time she saw a baby seal clubbed, and got really angry over the treatment of blacks in South Africa. Maybe she even bought gold Krugerrands on the sly.

Marshalling my best smile, I knocked on the lime-green door. No answer. I looked around the tiny front yard. The remnants of a garden stuck up like stubble blasted by bombs. Stacked to one side was a pile of pine planks. I was beginning to think stacks of lumber were a prerequisite for being an islander.

"You must be Mr. Finnegan," a voice said out of thin air.

It came from behind me. I turned and saw a woman, probably in her mid-thirties, holding an axe. She was wearing a heavy red plaid shirt that was too big for her, and soiled army dungarees. Her hair was long and fiery orange, her face ruddy and outdoorsy.

"Yeah," I said, eyeing the axe.

She saw where I was looking. "Need to chop up some wood. It's going to be cold tonight. Come out back with me."

I followed her into the back yard. There was a large bin of firewood, a pile of paving stones and tiles, a little lean-to that might have been a toolshed, and a couple of lawn chairs. It was still drizzling, and I was getting chilly in my windbreaker; it didn't look as if we were going in. I'd had high hopes for a coffee or hot chocolate, maybe even a slug of Scotch.

"Sit down, Mr. Finnegan," she said, motioning to one of the lawn chairs. "It'll just take me a few minutes."

She started splitting logs with the axe. I shivered when a gust of wind got under my jacket.

"You should dress more warmly, Mr. Finnegan," she told me, smiling mysteriously.

"That's what my mother always used to tell me."

"You should have listened to her. You should always listen to your mother."

Whack! went the axe. I couldn't help thinking about Lizzie Borden. Wasn't she a redhead, too?

"You didn't say what paper you wrote for, Mr. Finnegan." Whack!

"I'm a freelancer." Whack!

She whipped her hair over one shoulder and stared at me. "It's a beautiful day, isn't it, Mr. Finnegan?" I knew this had to be a friend of Carole's. They both gave me the creeps.

"A bit cold and wet, I'd say."

"Look around you. Take a deep breath. Can't you feel it?"

"Feel what?"

"Life, Mr. Finnegan, life. This is what life is about. Not where you just came from. Not that... place over there. Here." Whack!

I shifted uncomfortably in the lawn chair. "Yeah, it's beautiful. I feel like I'm way up north," I said, shivering.

"Exactly, Mr. Finnegan." Whack! "That's why we don't want to leave. This is our peace, our sanctuary. Our... sanity."

"You could always move to Muskoka or Haliburton..."

"Why should we?" Whack!

"There are people who still want to turn this into a park. That way everyone benefits."

"Another Centre Island? Never." Whack!

I shivered some more. If I'd smoked, this would have been the point where I'd have lit one up. Sharon probably wouldn't have approved, and that really made me want to light up. Instead, I watched her swing the axe. The top buttons of her shirt were undone, and every time she stopped to set up another log, I could see her breasts. When the axe wasn't winking at me, her ruby nipples were. Then I felt something rubbing against my leg. It was a big tabby with one eye, just like the one that used to live in that house I'd shared with Carole. How many one-eyed tabbies were there in the world?

"Just who are you, Mr. Finnegan?" Sharon Praeger asked suddenly.

I looked up. She'd stopped chopping wood and was standing over me, the axe dangling in one hand.

"What do you mean?" I asked, blinking.

"You don't act like a journalist. What are you? A city spy? A building inspector? We still get a lot of those."

"I'm a journalist, like I said. Honest."

She frowned and set the axe beside the stack of firewood she'd split. "Come on inside. I'll make us some coffee."

I smiled at that and got out of the lawn chair a little too quickly. I nearly stepped on the tabby. It hissed at me. We went in the back door of the chartreuse cottage.

"Take a seat, Mr. Finnegan," she told me. We were in the kitchen.

"Call me Mickey."

She smiled and put some water on to boil. I watched her as she ground some beans and took a Bodum coffee maker down from a cupboard. The Bodum went with the image, I guess. On one wall of the kitchen there was a giant poster of a baby seal about to be sent to its maker. On another wall there was a poster of a man in a cage, with something in Spanish printed below. The man in the cage had his fist clenched, and his head was bloody. Below that was a more recent poster of a giant west coast Douglas fir surrounded by chain saws. I could have sworn the tree was crying.

The kitchen was warm and pleasant. Lots of pine— the floor, the counters, the table and chairs. Lining the top of the cupboards— also pine— were rows of what looked like South American gourd vessels, mixed in with a few clay pots with jagged geometric designs etched on their sides.

When I finished scouting the kitchen, I watched Sharon's ass as she moved about at the counter. It was nice and round. Then I felt something rub against my leg again. This time it was a tortoise-shell cat with two eyes but no tail.

"What happened to his tail?" I asked Sharon as I scratched the cat behind an ear.

"We have to take care of the injured and the sick," she said, pouring the water into the Bodum.

"Yeah," I said. Did Sharon ever answer a question, even a simple one? I picked up a book lying on the table. It was a history of the Toronto islands.

"Well, here we are," she finally said, spinning around and coming over to the table with the pot of coffee and two mugs. "Would you like some cookies? I just made them this morning."

She went and got the cookies— chocolate chip— and then poured the coffee. I added some cream and sugar to mine, and we sat silently for a few minutes. Looking at her shirt, I could have sworn she'd unbuttoned it even more. The tops of her substantial breasts were visible. I coughed.

She eyed the book I was thumbing through. "I'm writing a biography of the man this island is named after— William Ward. He was quite a guy." She smacked her lips when she said that. "Back in 1862, when he was fifteen, he took his five little sisters out for a sail. The lake has always been unpredictable, and a sudden storm came up from nowhere and capsized the boat. Young William tried to save his sisters— Rose, the youngest at five, Jane, Cecilia, Phoebe, and Mary Ann, the oldest at twelve— but they all drowned. William would have, too, if he hadn't been rescued. Can you imagine the guilt he must have felt? Especially after his father had warned him not to and he went ahead, anyway? And the mother of those poor girls. They say she never really got over it. She'd pace up and down the shore of this island, not far from where we're sitting, as if she expected to see them come ashore some day. After all, the little girls drowned only a thousand yards or so from the Ward home.

"Well, young Bill went on to devote his life to saving others. He became the island's lifeguard and saved 164 people over the next forty or so years. He told a reporter in 1909 that ever since the terrible deaths of his sisters, 'I tried to help those in distress.' Bill did a lot of other things, though. He ran a hotel here, flouted the province's prohibition law and sold alcohol, was constable of the island, earned a reputation as a champion fisherman, grew strawberries the size of tomatoes in his garden, and kept saving lives practically up to his death in 1912."

I got the feeling from all this that Sharon had found the man for her; the only problem was that he'd been dead for more than eighty years.

"Well, Mr. Finnegan, enough of local history. Just what paper or magazine do you hope to sell your article to?" She batted her blue eyes at me.

I took a sip of coffee. The hot liquid was wonderful. "Actually, I'm not doing a piece on the islands." I wondered for a moment if she'd throw her coffee at me. But nothing happened. "I'm looking for someone, a friend of yours, Carole Rutland."

"Carole? Who are you? A cop?"

I laughed. "Far from it. I told you, I'm a journalist."

"You're doing an article on Carole?" she asked, confused.

"No, not really. I... I just want to find her."

"Why?"

"Do I need another reason? I'm curious. We journalists are noted for our curiosity."

Sharon munched on a cookie reflectively. She got a few crumbs on her upper lip, and I had an urge to brush them away. "You're sure you're not a bill collector?"

"Honest. Cross my heart and hope to die."

Chewing her lip, her pink little tongue flicking away the cookie crumbs, Sharon seemed to make up her mind. "I haven't seen Carole in a long time."

"Any idea where she might be living?"

"No, not a clue."

"I thought you were her friend."

"She's a thief."

"Pardon?"

"She stole my answering machine. She used to live here, and when she left, she stole my answering machine."

I blinked at that. "How did you meet Carole?"

"Donald Yates. We both know Donald Yates. He and I took a pottery class once. He'd met Carole at a restaurant. She was a waitress. They got chatting, and, well, you know..."

"Yates was her boyfriend?"

"Sort of. Anyway, Carole was looking for a place to stay for a few months during the summer about two years ago, and she moved in here."

"Did you see her after she moved out?"

"You bet I did. I wanted my answering machine back, and some tapes, too. Vivaldi and Schubert. She doesn't even like classical music."

"How did you find her?"

"She was staying with Donald."

"That must have been not too long before she moved into our house," I said musingly.

"You know, she denied stealing anything. I almost believed her. Stared me right in the face and said she could never do anything like that and that if I kept bothering her she'd take me to court. The nerve!"

"I guess that was the end of the friendship?"

"You bet. I did see her a few more times, though. You know, we had mutual friends and all." For some reason Sharon blushed, her face turning beet-red. "We did some... things together. But the last time I saw her, let's see, that was a few months ago. I was walking down Bloor Street near Honest Ed's, and there she was. She wanted to go for coffee and tell me about the new guy in her life, and about her new career as a fashion designer. But I was still steamed about my answering machine and didn't go with her."

"And Vivaldi," I added.

"Yes. Anyway, that was the last time I saw her."

"Exactly when was that?"

"June, I think. A week after my twenty-ninth birthday. That's why I remember." She batted her blue eyes at me again. I let the twenty-nine jazz pass without even raising an eyebrow.

"What about this new guy in her life? Did she tell you who it was?"

Sharon frowned, and the colour drained from her face slightly. "Uh, no, she didn't. It was probably nothing. Carole always had some new guy. Men really go for her, you know." She looked at me meaningfully.

"And I suppose you didn't get any kind of address from her?"

"Why should I? Listen, if you really want to find her, you should talk to Donald. He'd know."

"Where do I find him?"

"He works as a clerk at a store on Queen Street West. It's called Vathek. They sell old books and things."

I finished my coffee, patted the tortoise-shell cat on the head, and got up. "Well, you've been a great help, Sharon. Thanks for the coffee, and the cookies."

She stooped and swept up the cat in her arms, giving me another eyeful of nipple. "Don't leave. I mean, there won't be another ferry for an hour. I don't get guests very often."

"Thanks, but I think I'll shove off, anyway."

"Maybe you should still do an article about the islands," she suggested, stroking the cat as she led the way through her living room to the front door. "You know, you should think about living here. It's so..."

"Healthy?"

She frowned. I looked around the living room. Where a colour television might normally have been there was a massive stereo system— tape deck, turntable, compact disc player, giant speakers, the works. Colourful batik works hung on the walls. The chairs were wicker, and the couch was a futon. On the floor was a grisly Mexican rug splashed with a red-and-rust representation of Quetzalcoatl. I wondered what Sharon did for a living.

"I made that," she said, pointing at the rug. She reads minds, too, I thought.

"Nice," I said as she opened the door for me.

"I sell a lot of rugs and quilts and things over there." I must have looked puzzled because she added, "The city, Toronto."

"Nice," I repeated. I was in the doorway. She was leaning against the frame; the cat had leaped to the ground, happy to get outside. I stared at Sharon's breasts.

"They're nice, aren't they?"

"Huh?"

"The trees along the shore. They're very old."

"Oh."

"Are you sure you won't stay? I could make us lunch."

I zipped up my jacket and shivered. It was still drizzling. "Thanks, but I think I'll take a walk."

She pouted. "Maybe you'll be back? We could talk about writing. I thought I'd write an article about William Ward, kind of an appetizer for my book. Maybe you could give me some pointers."

"Maybe."

"You aren't married or something, are you?"

"No, I'm not." Not any more, I almost added.

"By the way, how did you get my address?"

"From a professor friend of mine in the U of T English department. Carole—"

"Professor?" she gulped, as if someone had dropped ice on her spine. Then she shut the door.

I stared at the lime-green door for a moment, thoroughly perplexed. Sharon Praeger must have one hell of a phobia about professors. I knew academics could be lethal, but usually people didn't run and hide at the mere mention of the word. Then I remembered the tango in the back yard with the axe. Who could say? Maybe Sharon went to the same moon school as Carole.

Shrugging, I headed over to the shore. I walked along the beach, a patch of mud flats and rushes. The lake, seemingly endless, stretched southward toward the States. It was rough today, and the waves were smashing hard against the embankment when I reached the concrete boardwalk that ran all the way to Centre Island. With the stripped trees, the burnt sienna swirl of leaves, the slap of surf, the scree of sea gulls, I couldn't help but think of Laura and all the fall camping trips we'd taken. She loved the outdoors. She'd have loved this island. It was funny how we'd never come out here when she and I had lived in Toronto together.

I walked faster. There was no one else around. I was getting wet, but I forged on. Laura and I had always had our worst arguments when we were camping. On our last trip we'd gone up to a national park at the tip of the Bruce Peninsula. It wasn't quite the fall, more like Labour Day weekend, but there had been a chill in the air. That first morning our tent had had frost on it.

We spent the weekend scurrying about the sheer cliffs that dropped suddenly into Georgian Bay. As always, Laura was a gazelle on the slick rock, while I lumbered behind, trying my best not to slip and end up shish-kebab-style on a white limestone spire far below. I can still see Laura scampering ahead of me, her long tawny hair bouncing in the mild sunlight, her lush body barely contained in a pink-and-green halter top and white short shorts.

It was far too chilly for what she was wearing, but she'd insisted, saying that it would be her last chance to do so before the temperature dropped. Later, in the tent that night, she was so cold I had to wrap myself around her for hours. Her teeth chattered so much that I thought they'd break right off.

Perhaps to keep warm, maybe because we were practically one body, we made love frantically, maniacally, as if our lives depended on it. Just after Laura spasmed with a titanic orgasm, the rain and wind started, and our tent was nearly swept away.

Somehow I managed to fall asleep during that wild night. When I woke up the next morning, I had a mouthful of nylon and my arm was still beneath Laura's back. Our tent had been flattened, and everything in it was soaked. As we pulled the misshapen mess together, both of us wet and miserable, the rain still falling lightly, we had our first argument of the weekend. It escalated into a verbal skirmish that continued throughout the day in fits and starts until finally exploding into an all-out Armageddon of words that drove us back to Toronto prematurely and enveloped us in frosty silence for days after.

Our last camping trip... and yet the thing I want to remember is hugging Laura harder and harder as she convulsed beneath me, the wind rising with each of my thrusts into her quaking body. And I want to remember her on the trail along the cliff, leaping over the many holes in the porous rock, her whole body a smile as it soaked up every bit of late-summer sunshine.

The rain was coming down more heavily. I swung off the boardwalk and headed toward the ferry dock, passing a big flock of Canada geese. There were gaily painted little boats in the channel separating Algonquin Island from the long arm of Ward's that I was on. Ancient poplars, oaks, maples, and weeping willows were everywhere. Woodsmoke filled my nostrils. Somewhere I thought I heard a woodpecker, or perhaps it was someone chopping wood. Maybe I'd stay, never go back to the city, I thought. Just stay here, always. Go back to Sharon Praeger's, knock on her lime-green door, have lunch with her, and... never leave.

But I didn't. I caught the next ferry back to the mainland and watched a lone sailboat bob and weave on the angry water. The boat made me think of Sharon's Bill Ward and his desperate attempt to save his sisters. I could identify with Bill. He'd fucked up big-time, even worse than I had. Maybe the guilt had driven him to a life of atonement. If so, he'd certainly more than evened the score— 164 to five. That was more than I could say for myself. I had a few corpses in my past, too. And it seemed I'd launched myself on my own lifesaving program. But I had a long way to go before I could sit down in ol' Bill's company.

Then I thought about Ward's mother pacing the shore night after night. A woman searching, hoping, never quite giving up, no matter how irrational the attempt. Surely a mother should know where her daughter is. Looking back at the low-lying island, I blinked. For a moment I thought I saw a wraith-like figure flit along the shore.

Shaking my head, I turned and took in the tall thrust of the CN Tower, decapitated by the mist, its lights blinking on and off, the city's concrete-and-glass toadstools floating and wavering around it as if in a bad dream. Back to the city, I thought. Party time. But it wasn't Jack Malone's party I was thinking of as the ferry docked. All I could think about was that damn answering machine. Why had Carole stolen it? What could a woman who had great difficulty keeping a phone possibly want with an answering machine?

STATION IV

It didn't take me long to get to Jack Malone's house. He lived in the Annex, near the university, a fashionable, much renovated, old residential section of the city. The walk through streets strewn with maple leaves brought back memories of scores of similar jaunts that Laura and I had taken when we'd rented a house in the Annex once upon a time. Ploughing through the mounds of musty leaves, I could almost feel Laura beside me, commenting on each house as we passed, noting a lot of gingerbread here, a stained-glass window there, some terra-cotta around a door, a particularly striking widow's walk. Almost, but not quite. It had only been a little more than two years, but it seemed like aeons. Kicking at the leaves the way I used to as a child, I wondered if it had ever really happened, if I had ever really known Laura.

A cold wind swirled around me, and I pulled up the collar of my pea jacket. Sharon Praeger would have been proud of me— I'd traded the windbreaker for something more substantial. Mom would have loved me, too, if she were still around.

When I got to Jack's house, I didn't go in; I just stood in front of it. I could hear music— jazz— playing, glasses tinkling, people laughing. The house was lit up like a torch. Lights blazed everywhere. It was one of those narrow Victorian jobs— three storeys, little verandahs, a sharply peaked roof, lots of terra-cotta trim, sandblasted red brick, slender windows. Jack's castle, I thought. I could see Brigit up on the widow's walk, looking out over the Annex, waiting for her husband to return from the tempests of academe.

I didn't want to go in. The lights, the laughter, the music— Dizzy Gillespie's "Salt Peanuts," I think— the sparkle, the people, I didn't want any part of it. I wanted my hideaway. For a moment I despised everyone in that house. If I'd had a Molotov cocktail or two, I'd have blown all their trendy, intellectual bonhomie to kingdom come. For a moment...

But I went up the stairs, anyway. Jack was in there, and Brigit. I knocked on the big unpainted oak door. Solid, like Jack. No batik for Jack. No Swedish furniture. No chrome. No blips and bleeps on the stereo. No branch-bank pseudo Jackson Pollocks on the walls. No imitation Quetzalcoatls for the masses. No Walkmans or chi-chi wine-tasting parties. No shiny, soulless art rock. No leather-panted, earringed minimalist rock songsters masquerading as poets in the bookcase. Everything Jack had was earned. Every book consumed and digested. Every possession lived. Jack was stripped wood, clean, hot jazz, metaphors soaked in his own sweat and blood. He liked Romantic poetry and Victorian novels, but not the fake stuff, not even the good guys faking it. He liked the basics— Thomas Hardy at his lyrical, elemental best; bebop and trad; African drum music; Byron staring himself in the face; Shelley with his pants down; Wordsworth before he became an old fart; Coleridge grabbing hold of cold, hard reality in the white-hot flame of madness. Jack liked fiery Mexican food, and he picked the Peking duck he wanted for his dinner, making sure he got every last ounce of it from soup to skin rolled in crêpes. He could juggle Santayana, Whitehead, Jung, Nietzsche, Schopenhauer, Spengler, and Kierkegaard without a hitch, and throw in Nicholas of Cusa and Marcus Aurelius for good measure. He could get you raving about Descartes and the mind/body split, bring in Spinoza's monism, and turn you inside out, then demolish both rationalists and your brain with Bergson's dualistic creative evolution. Jack liked the mad ones, the Marlowes, the Rochesters, the Kleists, the Gogols, the Poes, the Dostoyevskys, the Strindbergs, the Kafkas, the Lowrys, the guys who dug deep and came up with their own entrails. He—

"Are you going to stand there all night, Mickey?"

Brigit was standing in the doorway, amused.

"Composing a poem, perhaps?" she asked, chuckling.

I'd always liked that chuckle. She never giggled, just chuckled throatily. "Uh, no, just reminiscing," I finally said.

"Could have fooled me. I could have sworn you were having an epiphany about God. Anyway, it's chilly, so please come in."

I followed her down a long hallway. Brigit, as always, was a knockout. She had on a white cotton shift with lace trim around the neck and sleeves and at the hem. She looked like a vestal virgin. Her blonde hair floated around her head like a halo. Her feet were bare. If I hadn't been thinking about God before, I was now, and God was a woman and one of her names was Brigit.

We got to the end of the hallway and came into the dining room, packed with professorial types. Lots of tweed jackets with elbow patches, a few turtlenecks, some lady profs in muumuus, a caftan here and there, a couple of august greyhairs in dark suits, and a free-spirited kind of guy in body shirt and leather pants. The latter I recognized immediately— Patrick Page, resident Canadian poet and playwright, playing gay this week, it seemed.

"Mickey," Brigit said as we plunged into the intellectual sardine can, "I want you to myself for a few minutes. It's been a long time. Let's get a drink and find some place—"

"Far from the mouldering crowd?"

She chuckled. "Don't let Jack hear you making fun of Mr. Hardy."

When we got to the kitchen, I fished a Tuborg out of the refrigerator and Brigit helped herself to some punch, then we elbowed our way into the living room where we found an unoccupied corner.

"So," Brigit began, perching herself on the arm of a multi-cushioned maroon sofa, "what do you think Freud and Fliess were up to? Surely they weren't just palsy-walsy letter writers."

"Huh?" I peered at her, which gave me the chance to admire that lovely face. Everything was perfect except for a little scar near one corner of her mouth, which was twisted now in that peculiar smile she had, the lips withdrawing a bit, showing a sudden sunburst of white teeth. Her nostrils flared at the same time, and her green eyes crinkled, and once again I was on that leaf-littered street, walking hand in hand with— nothing. All this, I thought, and Brigit, too. Jack sure had it made. Jack had always had it made.

"There you go again," Brigit chastised, tapping my nose with a slender white finger. "You've picked up some bad habits in your hermitage. Freud and Fliess. Remember?"

And I did. The last time I'd seen Brigit we'd been arguing about Freud's personality problems. Brigit was a Jungian through and through, and as a woman, she was particularly miffed at Freud's rejection of the seduction theory. "Vat did vomen vant?" she'd once asked me in a mock-Viennese accent. "A varm, hot cock, of course, preferably unattached."

"I remember now," I told her. "You were saying something about Freud and Fliess having it off."

"Exactly! I wanted to know who'd be the pitcher and who'd be the catcher."

"Good God, Brigit, where do you get stuff like that?"

She batted her eyelashes. "Whatever do you mean?"

I sucked down some beer and looked at her again. Then I took another long slug. She was still there, a vision, waiting for me to say something trenchant. "I hear you're planning on doing a doctorate in Zurich," I finally said.

"No fair. You changed the subject."

"Still psychology, only more personalized."

She smiled. "Well, yes, I'd like to. Lots of logistics, though."

"Maybe Jack could get a sabbatical or something. He could work on a novel or two."

"There's Conor, too."

"He's little and not in school yet."

"You know, Freud might have had some weird Oedipal thing with Fliess."

I frowned. "Freud thought of Fliess as his mother *and* father? I thought that was Jung's problem with Freud."

"So Freud would have had everyone believe."

"How come you don't have any theories about the sexual relationship between Freud and Jung?"

"Jung spent most of his time in heterosexual overdrive," Brigit said with mock shock, running her tongue over her upper lip with obvious pleasure.

"Can I get in on this conversation?" a voice broke in. It was Jack. He wasn't wearing the corduroy jacket and work pants for a change, not even the cravat or the construction boots. Tonight he was sporting a pale blue suede jacket scattered with bald patches. The jacket went well with his beige corduroy Levi's and dingy white open-toed sandals.

"Where do you shop, Jack?" I asked. "At rummage sales?"

Jack sniffed and tried to look offended. "Of course not. I get all my things at Honest Ed's."

"Even worse," I said, laughing. "That's where it comes from before the rummage shops get hold of it."

"Will you listen to that, Brigit? I invite the guy to my book launch and he insults my clothing."

"You married me, and I insult it all the time," Brigit quipped.

"I wonder what Freud would have made of that," I added.

"Enough sartorial talk. What were you two talking about?" Jack asked.

"Oh, the usual," I told him. "Psychological patricide and the quest for unlimited sex."

"Charming. I suppose Brigit has been going on again about old horny Jung. Personally I prefer Wilhelm Reich."

"You do not, Jack!" Brigit cried.

"Now there was a man who knew what women wanted," Jack continued. "It's too bad he got into little green men, communism, and orgones."

"Little green men?" another voice piped up.

I turned around to see a tall sandy-haired man wearing a three-piece green plaid suit. His long, leathery face was lightly freckled, and he wore horn-rimmed glasses perched near the end of his sharp, thin nose.

"Garrett Macpherson," Jack enthused, "man of the hour, day, and night, holder of the fifteen-minute flame."

"I expect you're having me on," the newcomer ventured, the unmistakable prickle of a burr struggling to survive the straitjacket of his acquired Oxford accent.

"Garrett Macpherson?" I said. "The man who found the *Cardenio* manuscript?"

"Garrett," Jack broke in, "this is Mickey Finnegan, an old friend of mine. Well, not all that old, eh, Mickey?"

"I'm not on the sunny side of twenty-five any more," I said, feeling Jack was winding up his old patronizing machine. He used to love referring to my callow years, especially when I disagreed with him.

"Not to worry, Mickey," Jack said, grinning wickedly. "No one here is, either. But to return to introductions. Play your cards right, Garrett, and Mickey here, sunny side of twenty-five or not, will make you even more famous. He's a pretty hot reporter."

"Used to be," I corrected.

"Malone—" Macpherson began.

"Brigit," Jack interrupted, "let's mix."

Before I could say anything, Jack had left me with the tall, stoop-shoul-dered professor. The silence built a mortuary around us. Then I finally piped up, "I *am* quite interested in this *Cardenio* business, Professor." I always called professors "Professor." I'd even had a hard time kicking the deference-and-awe bit with Jack.

Macpherson eyed me morosely. "Malone obviously finds it all very funny."

"Any leads on the whereabouts of the manuscript?" I didn't want to get into any academic brouhahas.

"I'm not at liberty to say," Macpherson replied.

"I was surprised there was ever such a manuscript in the first place."

Macpherson took a short sip of what looked like a gin and tonic. Obviously he'd picked up bad habits at Oxford. He pushed his glasses up against the bridge of his bony nose in what was probably one of his standard gestures preliminary to launching into a lecture. "It was lost for centuries. There are records of its existence and a reference to its performance in Shakespeare's time, but not a line has come down to us."

"Until now," I put in.

"Precisely," he said, peering at me down the sharp ridge of his nose, perhaps wondering just how much Jack had rubbed off on me. "There is an adaptation of *Cardenio* by the eighteenth-century scholar Lewis Theobald called *Double Falsehood,* but it appears to have been a fraud. You see, there's been nothing like this. There *are* no Shakespeare manuscripts. That alone is something of incalculable worth— to have something, an entire play, in the hand of the greatest writer in the English language, perhaps the world!" Macpherson's eyes were glowing and his face was flushed.

"What's the play about?" I asked him.

If there was such a thing as an academic hard-on, the professor had one. "It's simply the find of the century. Think of it! A romantic comic plot derived from Cervantes's *Don Quixote*. The story of Cardenio, known as the Ragged Knight, and Luscinda, is actually a novella embedded in the novel. Don Quixote and Sancho Panza happen upon a half-naked wild man who has been roaming the remotest part of the Sierra Morena in terrible despair. They learn that he's been spurned by the beautiful, golden-haired Luscinda, who has married Cardenio's best friend, Fernando. As the story progresses, it gets more complicated, introducing another spurned lover, Dorotea, who has been jilted by Fernando.

"The tale rambles on, but eventually the spurned lovers concoct a scheme to get back their respective sweethearts, a plan that involves playing on Don Quixote's delusions of knight errantry. They do this mainly to lure Don Quixote out of his wild melancholy over Dulcinea, which he has invented, having borrowed the trappings of Cardenio's real desolation. So, you see, it has everything— frustrated love, destructive lust, madness, betrayal, a traitorous friend, slapstick, sexual mix-ups, burlesque, the possibility of real tragedy, even a woman, Dorotea, who disguises herself as a boy. Truly a pearl to set beside *The Winter's Tale* or *Cymbeline!*"

"And just how did you come across it?" I asked, ever the reporter.

"Not long ago the university bought a collection of manuscripts, letters, documents, and old books from an antiquities dealer in London. I went over to England to facilitate the shipment. We knew the contents of the collection to some extent, of course, but there were a lot of unknowns, as there always are, that would have to be patiently sifted."

"Kind of like a scholarly boodle bag," I cracked.

Macpherson's beady eyes nailed me. He looked like a giant parrot decked out in green plaid. He went on as if I hadn't said anything. "It took months, once I was back at the university, to catalogue properly the contents of our new acquisition. Nothing exceptional— a lot of flotsam and jetsam from the seventeenth century. The best thing in the whole assortment was a quarto of one of John Webster's lesser plays, and a collected works of Beaumont and Fletcher, published in the late 1660s. But we already knew about them.

"There was a curious leather portfolio containing anonymous seventeenth-century poems on vellum— pure doggerel. However, the front cover of the portfolio was in bad shape, and I thought I could feel something secreted inside it. You can imagine my excitement. I slit it open, and there it was— about a hundred pages of rag paper covered with a flowing secretary hand! It appeared to be a draft of a play, with numerous corrections. I read it that very night, taking great care with the fragile paper."

"And it was *Cardenio*?"

"Absolutely! Of course, it had to be authenticated, and that would take a long while, but I knew there and then that I had come across the most significant—"

"Find of the century," I interjected. It was beginning to sound like a litany at a benediction Mass.

Macpherson coughed, but he was too cranked up now to take offence. "Just think of it! A play written in Shakespeare's own handwriting! Good Lord, there are only a half-dozen signatures and three pages of an unfinished play called *The Book of Sir Thomas More* in Shakespeare's handwriting, and the latter is still conjectural."

"How did you know *Cardenio* was written by Shakespeare, let alone that it was in his own handwriting?"

Macpherson snorted. "I made my own analysis, and I was convinced. I immediately told Avery, Professor Brownlee, the head of our department, of my discovery, and he was as excited as I. That was two weeks ago, and now... Not a trace. It's totally gone." The excitement drained out of his face, and he looked gaunt and defeated.

"You didn't make copies?" I asked incredulously.

"We didn't have time," Macpherson croaked. It sounded as if he were strangling. "You just can't slap it in a photocopier. Special precautions have to be made."

"Where did you keep it, then?"

"In the Fisher Rare Book Library. The security was excellent, I assure you, and no one outside myself, Professor Brownlee, and one or two colleagues in the department even knew of its existence. I did contact some fellow scholars in England and the United States, apprising them of our possible find and inviting them to come to Toronto to corroborate my authentication of the manuscript. And then that beastly article appeared."

"Article?"

"In the *Globe and Mail* last week. I don't know how the news got out. It was impossible."

"Who wrote the article?"

"Larry... no, Jerry something or other. A German surname, I think. What does it matter?"

"Jerry Bauch," I said, whistling. If anyone could ferret out a secret, it would be him. "So, no copies, no trace, not a line, almost as if it never really existed," I added.

"I assure you, Mr. Finnegan, it did and does exist. I did take notes, a few snatches of lines. I can remember others. The play lives vividly in my mind."

"There have been a lot of hoaxes associated with Shakespeare over the years. Wasn't there some handwriting expert who claimed he'd found a Shakespeare manuscript? That was pretty recent, wasn't it?"

"That man was a charlatan. He had the temerity to insist that a manuscript in the British Museum, one they've had for decades, was actually *Cardenio*. I can assure you *my* Shakespeare is genuine. Good lord, Mr. Finnegan, next you'll be insinuating *I* took *Cardenio*."

"Did you? If it does exist, it'd be worth millions. I'm sure I read that a Shakespeare signature once sold for three million or so. That's a lot of bread."

I thought Macpherson was going to burst a blood vessel. Forget the parrot; he looked more like a boiled lobster now.

"Well, well, well, there you are, Garrett," a voice wheezed behind me suddenly. "I think Malone intends to read from his new book. Come now, you need to take your mind off all this dreadful *Cardenio* business."

Macpherson tried to pull himself together. "Professor Brownlee, um, this is... this is..."

"Mickey Finnegan," I said, turning to see the newcomer.

"Yes. This is our chairman, Avery Brownlee."

The bird in front of me was an old one, desiccated and wrinkled, a mummy in a grey tweed jacket and baggy charcoal trousers. He was bald except for a few white wisps girdling his dome like cirrus clouds. His eyes were bloodshot and yellowish, his nose a red sponge, a drinker's nose now petrified, his mouth a twitching white worm that seemed to have a mind of its own.

"How do you do, Mr. Finnegan?" he said, proffering a dry, chalky claw.

Reluctantly I shook his hand. "You knew about the manuscript, didn't you, Professor Brownlee?"

"Of course I did," he replied, looking at Macpherson, confusion in his mouldy face.

"Besides you and Professor Macpherson, has anyone else actually seen the play?"

"Actually—"

"Mr. Finnegan here is a friend of Malone's," Macpherson cut in, as if that explained a lot. "He's a newspaper reporter, a colleague of the fellow who wrote that abominable article about *Cardenio*."

Brownlee didn't seem alarmed by all that, and I wondered how long he'd been listening to our conversation. Casting a wan smile my way, he took Macpherson by the arm and said, "If you'll excuse us, Mr. Finnegan," then steered the Scot who drank gin out into the maelstrom of the party. I watched as the lobster and the mummy walked over to a group of what I presumed were fellow English professors, then, looking at my empty beer bottle, I went in search of another.

After I fished a Heineken out of the fridge— there weren't any more Tuborgs, and what the hell, I'm promiscuous when it comes to alcohol— I leaned against a convenient wall and watched the party tumble before me. Over in one corner Patrick Page was heavily embroiled in a loud argument with Myron Green, a Marxist philosophy professor who'd once run for Member of Parliament in Trinity-Spadina riding.

The last time I'd seen Patrick Page he was doing his Jack Kerouac beatnik bit, black beret, wispy goatee, and all. He'd recently published an article hailing Kerouac as a true Canadian, not only because his parents were French Canadians, but because his prose sang of Canadianism, whatever that was. Throughout the article, Page hammered home the fact that Kerouac, just before he died, was working on a novel exploring his French-Canadian ancestry.

Page's own book of poems, *Muskeg Mantras,* had garnered him some notoriety, thanks to its fusion of anti-Americanism and Eastern mysticism with maple syrup nostrums and musings on the spirituality of the polar bear. He'd gone on to found a Canadian drama company that specialized in bombastic blue-collar left-wing earnestness; naturally Page wrote most of the plays and starred in more than was healthy for himself or his audiences. But that was his past, a past that included picketing Frank Sinatra concerts, defacing cinemas that never exhibited Canadian films, and publicly burning *TV Guides* drenched in chicken blood.

The Sage of the North was still a militant Canadian— give him points for consistency— but he did move with the times. Now he deigned to notice a world beyond the Land of the Maple Leaf— no more fifty-year moratoriums on all things American— and he even criticized a Canadian play occasionally. But Page's real passion these days was the writing of a gargantuan cycle of poems revolving, or devolving, around Canadian flora and fauna, which keyed in nicely with the Iron John encounter group he conducted once a month in High Park regardless of season or weather. It seemed that instead of telling us what Canadians weren't, mainly not American, he now sought to tell us who we were, or at least what. He even got a Canada Council grant for it. My fondest hope was to find out some day that Page had actually been born in the States. It would explain a lot. My next fondest hope was to get out of Jack's house before Page started reciting "Beaver."

I tried to hear what Green and Page were on about, but all I caught was Page's growl about the Levantine un-Canadianism of Marxism and the need for freer markets, while Green bleated about the evils of NAFTA and the necessity for all good socialists to soldier on despite the collapse of communism. It seemed Page had forgotten his role of pseudo-gay poet and had taken on his old standby of reincarnated Jack Kerouac, especially the one given in later years to mouthing anti-Semitic rants and right-wing bunkum. Or maybe he wasn't playing gay. I'd heard Page had cut a record with a hip Queen Street West performance poet named Christopher Cardinal. Maybe the costume went with that image— new wave hip-hop urban prophet cum sylvan guru. Still, I wondered how his poems about polar bears, muskrats, loons, trilliums, and Douglas firs fitted in with the electronic caterwauling of Cardinal.

"Do you always suck on empty beer bottles?" Brigit asked me suddenly. People always seemed to be sneaking up on me lately. I looked at the Heineken bottle. Sure enough, I'd polished it off.

"I was thinking," I told her, looking down at her wonderful face.

"Why don't you get yourself another and we'll go up and see Conor? Would you like that?" she asked, one alabaster hand playing with her jade necklace. It was almost identical to one I'd given to Laura.

"Sure, but I think I'll switch to something stronger." I helped myself to some rye and tossed in a couple of ice cubes. "Let's go."

Following Brigit upstairs to the second floor, I couldn't keep my eyes off her perfectly shaped posterior. Here I was going to visit her child and all I could think of was... We got to the top of the stairs and entered a nursery. Conor had kicked off his blanket, and Brigit bent over the side of the crib to tuck him in securely. Even in the dim light her face glowed. Conor was a cute tyke, a massive head of blond curls already evident. Brigit kissed his fat cheek and straightened.

"Beautiful, isn't he?" she said.

"Yeah," I mumbled. An image of Laura flashed through my mind. I drained my whiskey and knew only one thing: I had to get out of Jack's house. "Brigit," I whispered, "I think I'm going to shove off."

She regarded me thoughtfully. "Jack hasn't read any of his stories yet. He's supposed to, you know, and he'd like you to hear them."

"I'm getting claustrophobia. I'm allergic to tweed."

She chuckled lightly, and we left the nursery. When we got downstairs again, she said, "Mickey, don't be such a stranger from now on."

"Sure."

"I mean it." Reaching up on tiptoe, she planted a lush kiss on my lips.

I was pretty sure I was blushing, and I definitely had a hard-on. So much for Sir Galahad, although I'd make a pretty good Lancelot. But wasn't Galahad Lancelot's son?

"Don't tell me I've embarrassed Mr. Tough-Guy Reporter."

"I wish people would quit calling me a reporter. I haven't written a real article in over two years."

"Are you okay?" she asked me, real concern on her radiant face. I might as well have been an older version of Conor.

"Yeah, I'm super-duper. Listen, Brigit, it was a slice of nice, but I've got to get going."

"You hated the party, Mickey. Tell the truth."

"Anything's worth the sacrifice to see you again, Brigit."

"Well, then, why don't you come to dinner next week? Just you, me, Jack, and Conor. No crowds."

"Thanks. I'll give you a call."

"Good. Make sure you do. Now I'd better get back to the party. Take care, Mickey. You have friends, you know."

I watched as she threaded her way through the party-goers. She floated in my alcohol-inflamed brain. I wondered if Jack had told her not to mention Laura. Mother and child, I thought. House with a big maple and a yard. Mother. Child. I shook my head and made a beeline for the front door.

"You're not leaving, are you?" Jack's Kennedyesque voice asked me. More than twenty-five years in Canada and he still sounded as if he ought to be playing touch football and kissing babies' bottoms on Boston Common. He grabbed my elbow and directed me to a corner of the vestibule.

"Yeah, you know me," I said, "parties get to me after a while."

"What did you do to Macpherson? For the past hour he's been glowering at me as if I'd suggested his tenure be terminated."

"Oh, I just asked him if he stole *Cardenio*."

Jack slapped me on the back and laughed. "You always knew how to make friends. He looks as if someone slipped him a castor oil mickey."

"Funny, Jack. Maybe you should call me James from now on. It is my first name, you know. By the way, Brigit let me see Conor."

"Cute devil, huh? Takes after his dad."

Why? I wondered, trading grins with Jack. Why did some guys have all the luck? Jack already had two daughters from a previous marriage. "Why?"

"Why what?" he asked me.

"Nothing. Just mumbling, as usual."

"Macpherson and Brownlee are camped in one corner like Cassius and Brutus plotting the overthrow of Caesar."

"That's what I like about you university types. Always quick with the literary stuff. Shakespeare, too. Nice touch."

"'And no two such as these, the clown and the buffoon, shall we see when comes the reckoning.'"

"Something suitably seventeenth century? Your old pal Thomas Fuller?"

"Nope. One hundred proof Thomas Moore."

"Who?"

"Well-known Irish Romantic. Friend of Byron. 'The harp that once through Tara's halls,' and all that."

"Sounds more like Shakespeare to me. It must be nice to have a quote on your lips at all times."

"My bedside reading every night is *Bartlett's*. Does wonders for your erudition."

Jack was grinning again. Laugh-a-minute Malone. But I loved the guy. I'd missed him a lot the past two years. I'd missed a whole lot of things.

"Listen, Mickey, I've been meaning to ask you how your search for Carole Rutland's going," he said suddenly, grin gone.

"So-so. I went over to Ward's Island and saw Sharon Praeger."

"Was she helpful?"

"She gave me another name— Donald Yates, another friend of Carole's. I'm going to see him on Monday."

"You're really getting into this, aren't you?"

"My hobby. Something to do. Idle minds, you know. By the way, I got the funniest reaction from Sharon Praeger when I mentioned I got her name from a professor in the U of T English department."

"Really? Did you tell her it was me?"

"I didn't get the chance. She froze up, as if I'd said something unspeakably obscene. Do you know her?"

"Never met the lady. Maybe she's like Carole."

"That's what I thought." I looked closely at Jack in the dim light of the vestibule. Cheshire cat Malone. Old, harmless, charming Jack, husband of a goddess.

> Hear me, hear me—
> Astarte! my beloved! speak to me:
> I have so much endured— so much endure—
>
> A future like the past. I cannot rest.
> I know not what I ask, nor what I seek...
>
> Speak to me! though it be in wrath;— but say—
> I reck not what— but let me hear thee once—
> This once— once more!

"What the hell's that?" I asked.

"Old Owen Clarke's giving his standard recital of Byron's *Manfred*. It's always a hit with undergraduates. Owen's a frustrated thespian."

> What I have done is done; I bear within
> A torture which could nothing gain from thinc...

"Such angst," I said.

"Go get 'em, Owen!" Jack cheered.

> Thou didst not tempt me, and thou couldst not tempt me;
> I have not been thy dupe, nor am thy prey—

"He's pulling out all the stops," I ventured over the roar of Clarke's thundering.

Back, ye baffled fiends!
The hand of death is on me— but not yours!

"At this rate I don't think I'll ever get to read one of my stories," Jack said. "By the way, Mickey, here's a copy of my book." He gave me a slim paperback— black with white lettering.

"Thanks."

"You'd better get going. After Owen's finished, Page is going to read from his work in progress."

'Tis over— my dull eyes can fix thee not;
But all things swim around me, and the earth
Heaves as it were beneath me. Fare thee well—
Give me thy hand.

Just as Clarke stage-whispered Manfred's final words, the lights went out all over the house.

"Neat trick, huh?" I heard Jack say in the gloom. "I wonder how he manages it every time."

"Bye, Jack," I said, grabbing my jacket.

"Keep in touch," he said.

I left the dark house, but stopped for a moment on the sidewalk. It was really cold— my ears felt in need of earmuffs— and I wondered if snow would come early. Rising over the tall, narrow Victorian homes in the midnight street was the CN Tower, its blue and red lights winking ferociously at me as if it knew something I didn't. From Jack's house I could hear the melancholic insistence of Shirley Horn singing,

You won't forget me
On nights like this
The moon will cast you
The shadow of my kiss
No matter where you are

With whom you are
You'll think of me
You won't forget me
Just wait and see.

Then Miles Davis's unmistakable trumpet in soul-piercing counterpoint. Turning my back on the Tower, I made my way down the street, kicking at the leaves as I went. It had been a long day.

STATION V

On Monday morning the phone rang at nine sharp. I was an unemployed wastrel, so nine was early for me. I struggled off my futon and tripped my way to the living room. The phone kept up its banshee act, and I only wanted to find a shoe or something to throw at it and stop its shrieking. But nothing was at hand. Answering it seemed less trouble.

"'Lo," I coughed into the receiver.

"Mickey, it's Jerry. I've been trying to get you all weekend. Where've you been? More important, whatever happened to your answering machine? Did you hock it or something?"

Not a bad idea, I thought. "I forgot to put it on. Anyway, Jerry, you ought to know better than to call me this early."

"Someone has to save you from yourself."

"Cute. Now that you've ruined my morning, what's up?"

"Did you hear about the Shakespeare manuscript stolen from the U of T?"

"Yeah. *Cardenio.*"

"That's the one. Well, I've been covering the story for the *Globe.* You know, jack of all arts gets to do the Woodstein bit."

"You phoned me at this ungodly hour to tell me you're auditioning for *All the President's Men II?*"

"Temper, temper. Haven't you got a friend who teaches English at the university?"

"So what?"

"I'm getting stonewalled. Since I did the piece about the discovery of the manuscript, no one'll talk to me. I wanted to get more information about *Cardenio* out of the guy who found it— Macpherson— but he's clammed right up. Same goes for the chairman— Brownlee. They act as if it's my fault the thing got snatched. Anyway, maybe your guy knows something."

"Sorry to disappoint you, Jerry, but Jack knows about as much as you and me. I was at a party at his place on Saturday."

"Sounds as if you were doing your partying last night."

"I just kept drinking right on through the weekend. It's kind of a tradition."

"Well, what about Macpherson and Brownlee? Could you pry something out of them?"

I must have laughed a little too loudly, because Jerry got awfully quiet. I could imagine him on the other end of the line, his fleshy lips draining of all colour, his skin blanching, his eyes becoming flinty, his great forehead tightening. No one got angry the way Jerry did. You felt the barely restrained violence for hours, sometimes days.

"You still there, Jerry?"

"In a manner of speaking."

"Listen, I'm even less popular with Macpherson and Brownlee than you are. I wish I could help you, but I don't see a way." I paused. As far as I could tell, Jerry had stopped breathing, too. "Shit, I'll tell you what. I'll check with Jack and see if he can nose around."

That seemed to mollify him; he grunted.

"Good," he said, "I can use all the help I can get."

"Do you have any idea who took it, Jerry?"

"I'm partial to Macpherson or Brownlee or both, but that might be construed as prejudice on my part. Macpherson's the kind of person who makes me proud I never trod the halls of ivy-infested academe."

"You're beginning to sound like me."

"Like you?" he snorted. "It seems to have slipped your mind that you *did* attend one of those places, or that you were made for elbow patches, a briar pipe, and windy dissertations about Swift's digestive system and its relation to Stella. If anything, my presence has finally begun to have some beneficial effect on you."

I ignored his barbs—you had to if you wanted to be Jerry Bauch's friend, and besides, he was only being playful. "You don't seriously think Macpherson stole it, do you? I'm betting he invented the whole shebang. I mean, who's to say otherwise? Brownlee? I think that bird's too topped up with formaldehyde to know the score."

"Don't underestimate Professor Avery Brownlee, Mickey. If there's a scam going on, he'd be behind it, not Macpherson. But forget about hoaxes and humbug. A couple of other ivory tower lads saw the mysterious *Cardenio,* too. It exists, and someone pilfered it."

"But a Shakespeare manuscript found in the cover of an old portfolio? C'mon, Jerry, that's the kind of thing you read about in comic books."

"My, my, we are stepping up our taste in literature, aren't we? Believe it or not, Mickey, the strangest things happen even outside the realm of Spider-Man and The Flash."

"Favourites of yours, no doubt."

"Not really. When I do read comic books, I only read the better ones. You know, vintage *X-Men* and *Silver Surfer.* Though lately I've gotten rather fond of *Cerebus the Barbarian.* It's done wonders for aardvarks. But sneeriously, to address your question about finding art in strange places. Back in the sixties someone found most of one of Menander's comedies wrapped around an Egyptian mummy. Yuh find yer artsy stuff wherever yuh can, pilgrim."

"I still think Macpherson and Brownlee aren't your boys," I said, smiling in spite of myself.

"Then who?"

"Beats me. Listen, why don't we get together, say, Wednesday? I'll see what I can do about Jack, and failing that, maybe we can pool notes."

"You writing an article on this *Cardenio* business, too? I don't share by-lines, you know."

"Why does everyone think I'm writing articles? I'm retired. You of all people ought to know that."

"Remember what Oscar Wilde said about women?"

"No, but I bet I'm going to find out."

"'Certain women should be struck regularly, like gongs.' Well, Mickey, you should stop getting it the other way round and quit beating yourself with women."

It was my turn for frosty silence, but I couldn't resist saying, "Noël Coward said that, not Oscar Wilde."

"Enough said. Advice to romantic journalists is like vaginal discharge to a devout Muslim— smelly, suspect, and definitely not to the taste."

"Christ, you can be goddamn vulgar."

"Thank you. Now, how about we meet at the Hole-in-the-Wall?"

"I've never heard of it."

"It's on Queen Street, just west of Bathurst. Wednesday. Eight. Okay?"

"I thought you hated Queen Street West."

"I do. Just think of this place as part of your ongoing education."

With that he hung up, and I was left holding a dead receiver. One thing both Jerry Bauch and Jack Malone had in common was their habit of abruptly hanging up. Part and parcel of being busy people with jobs, I guess. I was forgetting what that was like.

As I replaced the telephone receiver, another one of Jerry's irritating tendencies came to mind— his gibe about my reading habits had smarted, after all. Jerry could suggest you were an imbecile by loading you down with something that would never occur to you as a pastime, then adopt the pastime himself and act as if his indulgence in it was somehow that of a connoisseur, just as you were successfully dissociating yourself from the pastime altogether. In other words, he could heap sarcasm on the pinheads who lined up to see *Jurassic Park X,* then troop off to see *Attack of the Killer Kumquats* and find relevancy and resonance hidden from everyone else, including the writer and director.

Jerry's reviews for the *Globe*— he usually specialized in film and jazz, but seemed capable of forming an opinion on anything— were maddening. I used to think they were predictable, in that he could be counted on to champion something everyone else detested and vice versa, but just when you thought you had the guy figured, he'd pull a double whammy on you and detest something he should have liked or tout something he should have roasted. You might throw up at the thought of kumquats, but after reading Jerry's review of their star vehicle, you'd be hard-pressed not to rush out and pay big bucks for a ticket to the movie. And as if that weren't enough, two months later, when you yourself were raving about kumquats, Jerry would freeze you with a glare and demand, like some porcine version of George Sanders, say in *All About Eve,* how you could possibly stomach such unmitigated dreck, comparing the viewing of it to sticking your head in the hole of an outdoor shithouse somewhere on the outskirts of Lagos, Nigeria, on the hottest day of the year. No, Jerry was far from consistent, but he never raved Rex Reed fashion or resorted to thumbs up or down in the manner of vapid tele-critics like Siskel and Ebert. Instead, he argued with skill and savvy, and he could write. Christ, he could write!

More importantly, though, putting Jerry as critic aside, there was his loyalty. When things had come unglued for me, Jerry had stuck with me. He was still there, and I could count on him, always. Of course, friendship with Jerry did mean developing a thicker skin. He could be devastating, especially with his friends, and he had a lot of quirks, many of them unsavoury, though I suspected they were part of the armour he'd fashioned for himself in a world he viewed with distaste and distrust.

Resigning myself to being up before noon, I made some filtered coffee, ate a couple of petrified tea buns and, in a moment of nutrition guilt, drank a tumbler of orange juice. Then I took a shower, got dressed, and dragged myself out the door of my one-bedroom basement apartment, where it always seemed as if it were a quarter to midnight.

Outside it was one of those Indian summer days other people always tell you about but which you never seem to experience yourself. The hint of snow and cold fronts of the weekend seemed a mirage on a glorious sunny day such as the one that revived my spirits as I made my way by streetcar to Donald Yates's place of employment— Vathek, on Queen Street West.

In the soft sunlight the CN Tower soared stark and spare above the playfully decadent boutiques peddling nostalgia and camp and the chi-chi cafés heavy on art deco food and furniture on Queen West. Jerry detested this stylish strip, but its many used bookstores never failed to entice me. In my hermitage I'd become something of a bookaholic. In fact, I seldom ventured out these days unless it was to buy food, to cash unemployment cheques, see Jerry occasionally, or browse for books. Of course, now I had another hobby— hunting for Carole Rutland.

I could see what bugged Jerry about Queen West— it got to me, too, at times— but unlike him, I found more to appreciate in the curious mélange of skid-row tacky and spaced-out trendy. You could get anything you wanted here— bargain furniture, cyberpunk haute couture, minimalist macramé, wicker baskets, buttoned-down attaché cases, sexy leather whips, tie-dyed candles, five-and-dime da Vincis, secondhand windsurfing equipment, Levolor blinds, artwork that pogoed with the best in the thrash pit of yesterday's newest wave, books, of course, and even the potpourri of a Goodwill store. Or you could eat tuna melts and drink Perrier in a dim café where the waitresses wore lots of black eye shadow, had Day-Glo hairdos or shaved skulls, and seemed to be resurrected zombies from a Paul Morrissey horror flick; hoist a few pints in a beer parlour where time stood still, stuck somewhere in the 1940s, and the patrons, mostly men, wore furtive looks and two-day-old beards while playing table shuffleboard or darts; and wolf down greasy souvlaki and greasier french fries in an old Toronto tradition, the open kitchen, the kind of place where the coffee supported the mug it came in. No, Queen West wasn't Greenwich Village, Covent Garden, Les Halles, or even Toronto's Yorkville, though maybe it was trying hard to be a deconstructed, postmodern alternative to the latter's smug, high-priced swank.

I'd been down here countless times, but I'd never noticed Vathek. It was a small shop near Spadina, sandwiched between a Cajun food bistro and a computer store. The shop's facade was a real hoot. It had been built to resemble one of those mouths of Hell that medieval artists loved so much. As I made my way past the oversized fiend's fangs, I couldn't help shivering. Inside it was stuffy and dim, and maybe not all that unlike Hell. I stood there, letting my eyes adjust to the scarce light. The place didn't have any windows, and with the monster mouth out front, daylight had a hard time penetrating.

When I'd pushed open the door, a little chime had rung out, but so far no one had materialized.

"May I help you?" a voice finally asked.

I spun around but couldn't see anybody. Then, from behind a large cabinet, a tall, thin, silver-haired man emerged.

"Just dusting," the man said. "Never any peace from the dust in a business like this."

"Uh," I mumbled, my eyes riveted on the African masks housed in the black-and-red lacquered cabinet he'd been obscured by. They were almost as horrific as the mouth adorning the shop's facade.

"We have just about anything you could possibly want," the silver-haired man said, by way of assisting my aphasia as he gave me a toothy smile.

Though his hair was slickly silver, he wasn't that old. His face was relatively smooth except for crow's-feet around eyes the same colour as the ebony masks in the cabinet. And he looked pretty fit in his smartly tailored charcoal suit, white shirt, and blood-red tie. Everything he had on had the look of silk, even his hair.

"Uh," I stammered, "I... I'm not actually looking for anything."

A tight little smile flickered on his thin lips. I was pretty sure he knew I couldn't afford to buy a doorknob in his place. He was beginning to resemble a well-fed ghoul. There was something about the combination of toothy smile and bloodless lips, and I noticed wrinkles around his mouth, which made it pucker a bit. I now guessed him to be in his late forties, maybe early fifties.

"Actually, I'm looking for someone— you *are* the owner?"

He nodded.

"Someone employed by you, at least I think he works here."

"And your name?" he asked in an upper-class English accent.

"Oh, I'm sorry. Ever since I came in here my brain hasn't been functioning properly. Mickey. Mickey Finnegan."

"Well, Mr. Finnegan, are you going to tell me whom you wish to see?"

"D-Donald Yates." The man unnerved me, as if I were developing instant Alzheimer's.

"Perhaps it's the air," he said, blinking those startling jet eyes.

"Pardon?"

"Many of the things in my shop are very fragile and valuable, so the air temperature and humidity have to be rigidly controlled. It sometimes throws people off. Now, as for Donald Yates, yes, he works here. He's in the back. If you'll excuse me, I'll go fetch him. Why don't you take a look around? You might find something you like." He smiled faintly, as if there were a disagreeable odour in the room, then disappeared behind a black curtain.

He was right about the air. As I took a quick tour of the place, I felt as if I were running a marathon on Mount Everest. No wonder I was disoriented.

Vathek had everything— ashtrays fashioned out of elephant feet; Zimbabwean soapstone carvings of hippos, giraffes, and the like; plumed war shields from Canada's Pacific coast; jade tigers from Sri Lanka; shrunken heads from the Amazon; Haitian voodoo dolls, pins in their heads, hearts, and crotches; a blood-stained shirt reputedly worn by Robespierre on the day his friends guillotined him; Russian icons depicting particularly gruesome crucifixions; a marble bust of a young man that could have been by Bernini but wasn't; gold Celtic torques; a horrific stone Sheila-na-gig, its stubby hands prying its monstrous vagina ever wider; dainty ivory netsukes from Japan; tiny Aztec children's wheeled toys made from clay; iron thumbscrews from medieval Germany; and, looming in a corner, a malevolent-looking Spanish iron maiden courtesy of the Inquisition. And there were books: first editions of the Marquis de Sade, Aleister Crowley, Madame Blavatsky; a seventeenth-century Bible; a first edition of de Lautréamont's *Maldoror,* a scarlet-and-black leatherbound *Venus in Furs*; a tattered copy of the witchfinder's manual, the *Malleus Maleficarum.* The beautiful and the beastly.

"All they need here are some Nazi lampshades made from human skin," I muttered out loud.

"I'm sure we could oblige," the voice of the owner piped up behind me.

Tearing my eyes away from a particularly bloody painting of an accused witch having her breasts removed with red-hot pincers, I turned to see the silver-haired geezer standing with a blond guy in the archway leading to the back room.

"Mr. Finnegan," the silver-haired owner said, "this is Mr. Yates. Now, if you'll excuse me, I have a great deal to do." With that he spun on his heel and slipped behind the curtain. Probably going to unload his latest crate of cadavers, I thought.

"Do I know you?" the blond guy asked, puzzled.

He was around six feet, had a smooth suburban face, and was stuffed into an expensive pair of pleated taupe slacks and a loose-fitting crew-necked canary-yellow sweater. When he slid the slender fingers of his left hand over his short, receding blond hair to pat it down, I got a glimpse of his wrist, which sported one of those watches supposedly chipped from the Matterhorn or something. Donald Yates looked awfully pretty and terribly familiar.

"No, you don't know me, really," I finally said.

He wiggled his neat eyebrows at me, and I swear, twitched his nose like a rabbit.

"We do have a mutual acquaintance, though," I rushed in before the confusion turned to consternation. "Carole Rutland."

He stopped twitching his nose and narrowed his pale blue eyes at me. For a moment I thought he might have stepped out of *The Great Gatsby*. All he needed was a pencil-thin moustache. "Carole. Ah, yes, Carole. I haven't seen her in quite some time."

"Quite some time," I echoed. "How long's quite some time?"

"Why are you looking for Carole?"

"Did I say I was looking for her?"

"Well... I mean... aren't you?"

"That's beside the point." I looked at him hard, wondering if old Sharon Praeger, she of the wonderful tits, had tipped him off to my coming. "Yeah," I said, "I'm looking for her."

"May I ask why?"

"I'm a little concerned about her, that's all. She seems to have disappeared."

"How do you mean?"

He was a great one for questions. "How do I mean? Why, do you know where she is?" I figured we could keep asking each other twenty questions all afternoon.

"I told you, I haven't seen her in... well, in at least a couple of months. No, it must have been longer than that. Let me see..."

"Try June."

"Why, yes, June. How did you know?"

"Took a wild guess. I'm good at stuff like that."

I had a fix on the guy now. I'd met him before. I'd gone out with Carole once or twice, and one of the times we'd gone to an English-style pub in Cabbagetown. She'd brought the blond anyone-for-tennis type along for the ride. They'd talked Japanese all night while I'd guzzled pint after pint of Smithwicks. Yeah, that's right, Japanese. I'd had the temerity to ask Carole what gobbledygook she and he were gibbering and she'd said Japanese. Donald old boy had just bobbled his neat little blond head and continued with his bad impression of Sessue Hayakawa, the prison commandant in *The Bridge on the River Kwai*. Such was a night out with Carole Rutland. Actually, I thought they'd been talking Martian.

"Listen, Yates, no one seems to know where Carole is. Doesn't that bother you? I mean, after all, aren't you her boyfriend?"

"If you knew Carole as you claim to, you'd know that's Carole. She's a free spirit. She comes and she goes."

"Yeah, and she speaks swell Japanese, too."

"Pardon me?"

"Skip it." Obviously she and he hadn't been speaking in tongues lately. "Don't you have an address or something? How do you reach her? Or have you broken up?"

"We have a relationship that goes beyond mere boyfriend and girlfriend. If Carole wants to see me, she just, well, sees me."

"Great. You haven't seen her all summer. You don't have her address. Doesn't that worry you a bit?"

"I told you...?"

"Mickey Finnegan."

"I told you, Mr. Finnegan, Carole does as she pleases. We have that kind of friendship. Obviously it's something you wouldn't understand." He sniffed when he said that.

I didn't get a chance to say anything else. Too bad. I wanted to ask him how the weather was on Mars. But the silver-haired owner came back into the room. He had a hard-looking character with him, a guy wearing a shiny, close-fitting black sport jacket and stovepipe pants. The new guy had red hair cropped short at the sides and a little longer on top. Mean was the word for him. Real mean, from his green eyes, sharp enough to cut your fingers on, all the way down his lean, tense body to the black stiletto boots on his lethal feet. I'd met Nik Rorke before, and I wasn't ready to meet him again.

"I trust you and your friend are having a nice chat, Donald," the silver-haired gent said as he headed for the door with Rorke.

"Yes, thank you, Mr. Shaw," Yates squeaked, one very white hand taking a swipe at his already immaculate hair.

"Good. I'm going out for a bit, but I'll be back before three. Be a good chap and uncrate that new shipment of German woodcuts for me." He turned to me. "You'd adore these woodcuts, Mr. Finnegan. They're part of a sixteenth-century series portraying Inquisition tortures. Very graphic. They'll fetch quite the price, I daresay."

"Indubitably," I said. "Listen, you got any saints' relics, say, St. Peter's testicles, a kidney stone belonging to Mary, or maybe some of Christ's navel lint?"

Shaw bared his teeth. No one would have called it a smile or a grin. "You're very humorous, Mr. Finnegan. Isn't he humorous, Nik?"

"Yeah, a regular Woody Allen."

"Good day, Mr. Finnegan," Shaw said. "Perhaps we'll see each other again soon. Come on, Nik, we've got work to do."

When the door closed behind them and the chime finished its song, I turned back to Yates. "Here's my phone number, if you happen to have a memory attack in the next few days and come up with some ideas about Carole's whereabouts." I scribbled the number on an automatic bank teller receipt and gave it to him. Who cared if he knew my bank balance? I was thinking of putting up a billboard to advertise it, anyway.

"Tell me, Mr. Finnegan, if you do find her, what then?"

He had me there. What then? I really didn't know. "Then I don't worry any more."

"Has someone asked you to look for her?"

"You mean, am I a detective or something?"

"Well, are you?"

"Hardly. I'm just a poor unemployed slob with too much curiosity for his own good."

"You must like her," he said thoughtfully.

"Yeah. You know, it's funny, but I guess I do, even if... even if she's a bit..."

"Different?"

"Yeah, different."

"Carole is one of those rare souls, Mr. Finnegan. I'll agree with that. It seems she was very lucky when she met you in that house."

That cinched him. I hadn't told him about sharing a house with Carole. He knew damn well who I was. Maybe even remembered the Japanese night.

"Your boss," I said. "Shaw, is it?" It was time for a new direction.

"Yes, Mr. Shaw."

"He got a first name?"

"Cedric Shaw."

"Mr. Shaw's got a humdinger of a shop here," I said, glancing around.

"Yes, we deal in just about everything."

"I bet you do. Well, don't forget. Let me know if you think of something."

"Of course. If I see Carole, I'll tell her to call you."

"That'd be nice."

When I got outside on the street again, I felt like puking. All I could think of was Nik Rorke. He was from a past I'd tried to forget with the help of a few truckloads of beer and a distillery or two of rye. One flash of Nik Rorke and it all came tumbling back. My days at the paper, the salad days, the days when Laura'd be there when I got home, the days when I was a political reporter digging up dirt and getting paid gold for it. Rorke hired out to anyone with the right cash back then. Still did, no doubt, though maybe he wasn't freelance any more. Rorke got things done for you, and back then, as always, there were plenty of politicians, building contractors, real estate developers, all kinds of guys and gals who had things that needed doing.

"What's the matter with you?" a deep voice rumbled at me.

The big cop in the beige car coat was standing in the doorway of the computer store. He had his brown fedora on, and it had a few more dents in it since the last time I'd seen it.

"Are you following me?" I asked testily, wondering if I'd developed a death wish in Vathek. This cop could have hammered me into the gutter merely by sticking out his substantial jaw.

"I could ask you the same question, fella. I got a reason to be here. What's yours?"

"Since when is it against the law to shop on Queen Street?"

"What makes you think I've got something to do with the law?"

"You don't look like a street cleaner to me."

"Depends on your perspective. Seeing as you know about the *Cardenio* business, seeing as you have a pal at the university, you ought to know a cop like me has a lot of footwork to do in a case like this. Checking out stores that might deal in something like an old manuscript's just one of those little chores."

"Why tell me?"

"Maybe you know something. You used to be a pretty good reporter, I'm told."

"You've got me at a disadvantage. You seem to know who I am. Who the hell are you?"

The cop grinned. Now that I'd had a better look at him, he wasn't all jug ears and beef. He looked as if he'd been beaten over the head with a baseball bat a few times, but he looked human. Big human, but human.

"Frank Kaplan, detective sergeant, Toronto police. Like my badge number, too?"

I gave him a grin. Support your local police department. Be kind to a cop day. What the hell was going on? I'd set out looking for a girl let loose from the asteroid belt and now I was consorting with the likes of Nik Rorke and a cop named Frank Kaplan.

"You might want to look real close at this place," I said, indicating Vathek. "One of the employees seems to be Nik Rorke."

"Yeah, I know. I saw him come out."

"Course, the geezer who owns the place has to have someone help sew the stiffs together."

"Huh?"

"You know, a little electricity, lots of fancy gizmos, a couple of fresh corpses from the nearest cemetery, a little help from Igor, and presto!"

"See what you mean. When it comes to corpses, Nik certainly knows which end's up. If I were you, Finnegan, I'd step lightly around that guy. By the way, what were *you* doing a week ago, say, last Tuesday night?"

"That when *Cardenio* was swiped?"

"That's what we figure."

"You flatter me, Sergeant. I don't get to be a suspect often, and I don't even have an alibi, unless you call a two-four an alibi."

"I thought you were retired."

"Only in a manner of speaking."

"Keep it that way, Finnegan. Watch your step," he growled as he hauled himself out of the computer store entranceway and cement-mixed down the street to a black sedan one tire away from junkyard nirvana.

Spoken like a true cop, I thought. Palsy-walsy, then boom! I just wanted to crawl back to my cellar. I hadn't had a drink all day, and though I never seemed to get drunk, a talent Laura had always admired, I could certainly blur the edges nicely. I wasn't getting anywhere with the Carole Rutland thing, but everywhere I went *Cardenio* was sure to follow, or was it the other way around?

Looking back at the fiery maw of Vathek, I remembered one of the times Carole had spent the weekend sobbing to herself. At some point she must have called a friend, because she was talking to someone other than herself, and I'd heard that someone clunk his way up the stairs to her room. That someone had been male. Donald Yates? Whoever he'd been he'd stayed the night, and I wondered if they'd made Martian love.

My cave beckoned.

STATION VI

BODY FOUND ON BEACH

The nude body of a woman identified as Sharon Praeger was discovered yesterday washed up on Kew Beach.

Staff Sergeant John Walker of the Toronto Police Department homicide squad said the body was discovered by two boys who live nearby. The victim had been struck repeatedly with a blunt instrument, possibly a hammer. At the present moment, the police have not confirmed if the victim was also sexually assaulted.

When asked if the Praeger murder might be linked to a series of brutal murder/rapes in the city recently, Staff Sergeant Walker declined to comment.

Since last fall, four women have been bludgeoned to death with what the police believe to be a hammer. All four were savagely raped. The cases remain unsolved.

Ms. Praeger, possibly the most recent victim of this killer, lived on Ward's Island, where she was a vocal leader in the islanders' fight to maintain their homes in the face of attempts to turn the residential sections of the islands into parkland.

An inquest into Ms. Praeger's death is to be held after an autopsy has been completed. Further details will be released at that time.

The front page of the *Globe* was propped against a jar of strawberry jam on my kitchenette table. I stared at it long and hard. A grainy photograph of Sharon Praeger accompanied the terse article. It must have been an old one— she looked ten, maybe fifteen years younger. With her red hair cut close to her head and an impish smile dancing on her lips, she seemed like a boyish pixie, not the earthy siren I'd encountered on Ward's Island on the weekend. Sharon murdered?

After I'd gotten up, I'd gone to the corner store to get some coffee cream, and the newspapers had been there, blaring much the same headline. BEACH BUTCHERY, one had trumpeted. KILLER CLAIMS FIFTH? another had squawked. And the *Globe,* more discreet as usual, not giving it top headline, but an edge to the article still— BODY FOUND ON BEACH.

My eyes kept going from the paper to the cereal box beside it. "Nude body... win a trip to Disney World... repeatedly with a blunt instrument... save decals of your favourite Disney characters... series of brutal mur-der/rapes... just think, Dumbo, Donald, Goofy... bludgeoned to death... dinner with Mickey and Minnie... after an autopsy has been completed."

I could hear myself laughing, and I pushed the cereal box aside, wondering crazily what beer would taste like on bran flakes. Stuck away as I'd been, I really hadn't been paying much attention to the string of grisly murders that had terrorized women in the city the past year. There was fear in Toronto, and the article before me certainly wasn't going to lessen it.

I read the piece over and over as I sucked up coffee. Sharon Praeger hammered to death? It couldn't be. My apartment was cold, but I might as well have been in a boiler room. Sweat trickled in every corner of my body, and I was starting to get the shakes.

My mind jerked back to Saturday. When I'd gone over to see Sharon, I'd been in a really cynical mood. Christ, I'd been cool, smug, superior, looking at her South American gourds, her quasi-Quetzalcoatls, her colossal stereo, her little bit of the North in downtown Toronto. But she believed in something. Had believed. And now she was dead. Murdered?

I reached over, pulled open the fridge door, and lifted out a Carta Blanca. Beer for all occasions, that was me. Mexican suited Ms. Praeger fine. I didn't have any Nicaraguan, which was too bad, otherwise I'd really have been in the right spirit. Yeah, spirit. Up the Sandinistas! Start the revolution! Christ, I was cynical. A true son of my era. I looked at the clock on the wall. Eleven-thirty. I ought to get one of those Mickey Mouse wall clocks. Maybe if I got the right cereal box I could write away for one. Shit! Usually I waited till past noon on the liquid refreshment, but what the hell.

Prying off the cap, I downed half of the bottle and glanced at the article again. The reporter who'd written it didn't seem to have any doubts about the nature of Sharon's murder, but I wanted to get some solid facts if I could. I thought about going down to the morgue to see what the good people there could tell me, but morgues and hospitals do funny things to me, and besides, no one there would tell me anything. That left Frank Kaplan. He was the only cop I might squeeze some information out of. He wouldn't like it, but he might tell me what he knew, or at least some more details.

Sharon Praeger murdered? I shuddered and drained the beer. It had only been four days since I'd seen her, and try as I might, I couldn't shake the feeling that my visit had had something to do with the article that kept shouting at me from the kitchenette table. So I got off the chair and headed for the living room and the phone. If I didn't keep busy, I'd spend the day drinking Carta Blanca and whatever else I could lay my hands on. It took me a while— I didn't know what division Kaplan inhabited— but I finally got him on the phone.

"You again," he said by way of greeting.

"Listen, Sergeant," I began, "I was reading the paper and—"

"How nice of you to call and tell me."

It was going to be tougher than I'd thought. "The Praeger thing. You know, yesterday's murder, the body found on the beach. Could you tell me anything about it?"

"Finnegan, we keep conversing like this and someone might think we're buddies. How the hell would I know anything about the Praeger killing? I'm Robbery, not Homicide. It didn't even happen in my division."

"The papers seem to think it's related to other murders."

"And you don't? That what you're trying to tell me?"

"I don't know. It just stinks."

"It stinks, does it? What's going on, Finnegan? You taking up police work? First *Cardenio,* now this Praeger woman."

"*Cardenio*'s got nothing to do with me, but Sharon Praeger does."

"You knew her?"

"I met her for the first time on Saturday." I'd almost said last time.

"Yeah?" Kaplan was interested now.

"C'mon, Sergeant, I'm sure you know what I've been doing lately. You don't seem to me to be the kind of guy to miss any tricks."

"You're looking for some woman named Carole Rutland and now you're poking into a murder. You also seem to be pretty nosy about a certain missing manuscript. A regular one-man police force."

"Sharon Praeger was a friend of Carole Rutland. That's why I went to see her."

Kaplan was silent. He was hooked. "Maybe you should be talking to Homicide."

"Maybe, but what have I got?"

"You've got something else. Spill it."

"Donald Yates. You know, the pretty guy at Vathek."

"Yeah."

"He's a friend of both Sharon and Carole. That's why I was visiting him."

This time the silence didn't seem as if it would end. "You still there?" I finally asked.

"Yeah. Okay. So you got a missing friend. You got a dead friend. What's it add up to?"

"You tell me."

"Homicide's pretty tight-lipped about this one, Finnegan. There's a lot of heat on them. Four, now five murders, and no leads."

"None at all?"

"Zip. All they know is the guy likes to tenderize them with a hammer."

"They're sure about the hammer?"

"Yep. Forensic says same hammer, too."

"What about Sharon? Same hammer again?"

"Don't know yet."

"Will you let me know?"

"Finnegan, what the hell are you doing? You think the Praeger murder's related to your friend's disappearance, but what's the connection? Sure they're friends, but Christ, haven't you heard of coincidences?"

"All the time. If it's the same hammer, I'll buy it."

"Let me get this straight. You think somebody's made the Praeger thing look like the work of the same wacko who stiffed the other four women?"

"Sergeant, I don't know anything. I don't know who killed Sharon Praeger. I don't know who killed those other four women. And I don't know where Carole is."

"Ever thought she might be part of the series?"

Now it was my turn to choke up. "Will you let me know about the Praeger thing, Sergeant?"

"Sure. But, Finnegan, you stumble onto something about this *Cardenio* business, you let me know. Okay? No fancy stuff, either."

"What makes you think I'm going to trip over *Cardenio*?" I asked, a chuckle in my voice. "Hell, I'm not a cop, remember? I'm supposed to watch my step."

He laughed, if you can call a noise like a landslide a laugh. "You seem to have a talent for bumping into crime, Finnegan. I'll let the Drug Squad know you're on the job."

"Oh, one other thing, Sergeant. Was Sharon Praeger raped?"

Kaplan's rumbling laugh stopped abruptly. "Yeah," he muttered.

"And the others. The paper says they were savagely raped. What do they mean?"

"Christ, Finnegan, what does it matter? They're dead, aren't they?"

"What does it mean, Sergeant?"

"It means what it says— savage, like an animal... like every awful fucking thing you could do to a person... to a body. Satisfied?"

I coughed.

"Look, Finnegan, I'll see if I can get a line on Carole Rutland, too. Okay? Keep in touch."

We hung up, and I sat back on the couch and glanced around my living room. Not much to look at. A lot of bookcases, heavy on literature, art books, and biographies— I was nuts about other people's lives— leavened with a little philosophy and psychology. A banged-up stereo with ten-dollar speakers. A cheap print of Edvard Munch's *The Scream*. Real cheery. Went well with my burnt orange furniture, ivory walls, and milk-chocolate rug. The few plants I had hanging near the window were almost as brown as the rug. I'd seen better-looking vegetation in pictures of the Sahara.

I felt better now, though. No urge to drain the fridge of beer. It was time to touch the next base in the ongoing search for the mysterious Carole Rutland. I needed an address to work on, and if friends couldn't help me, maybe Warren Crane, landlord par excellence, could supply the address Carole had moved to when Warren had turfed her out. I had hoped I wouldn't have to see Warren again, or my former residence. They still spooked me. But now I had no choice. With some sort of address in hand, I could follow the trail of Carole's hideouts, the yellow brick road, so to speak, and finally find Dorothy. If nothing else, maybe I'd get warmer. Right now I was stone cold.

The house on the park, the hellhole where I'd hit rock bottom, wasn't very far from my newer, cleaner hideaway. After a fifteen-minute walk, I found myself across the street from the building I had studiously avoided for a year and a half. I'd only lived in that lowering pile of yellow brick and Victorian gingerbread for a mere six months, but it had scored me for life.

It wasn't just the other bottom-of-the-barrel people I'd met there, and with severance pay from the *Globe* and some savings, I wasn't on welfare or unemployment as everyone in the house seemed to be, no, what shook me to the core had more to do with a screwed-up self-image and the loss of Laura. Punishing myself? Perhaps at first. I certainly didn't have to live in that brick-and-wood nightmare. Later, of course, it seemed as if I'd never get out, and when I did, the first few months in my present apartment were almost as hellish, because by that time financial necessity had been added to spiritual despair, though at least I'd freed myself of other people's misery.

Ensconced in my nice dark little basement, I no longer had to battle vermin, berserk fellow lodgers, collapsing ceilings, ruptured pipes, sporadic fires, or the constant din of too many unhinged people packed too tightly into a structure that defied gravity by remaining erect. Even when there wasn't actual noise in that house, it was implied. Madness and its handmaidens, fear and desperation, slithered through dustball-choked hallways, oozed out of mildewed walls, and rattled under warped floorboards, though the latter might have been mice, of which there were veritable legions.

The first while in my new apartment was tough until I got a security job, a mode of employment that only increased my quiet desolation. I worked in a small hospital for the recently paralyzed, a perfectly symbolic place for an emotional cripple to earn his daily bread. I lasted there five months, toiled as, believe it or not, a gravedigger for several more months, and then retreated farther into my cave to collect unemployment, a circumstance I still find myself in.

But I was free of the real and imagined lamias and leviathans that lurked in the house looming across from me at the moment, anesthetized against the pain of losing Laura, no longer tempted to find ever more distasteful employment as, say, a septic tank swabber, a stoker on a derelict Liberian freighter or, savouring the less dirty but more mindless, a switchboard operator for a pizza chain specializing in thirty-minute delivery. Hell, I even wrote the occasional article for obscure industrial publications— wonderful pieces extolling the virtues of extruded plastic or the subtleties of Gyproc. What was more, I had a new purpose in life— to find Carole Rutland.

Still, I stood there. The house had changed only in that it was even in greater disrepair. Hunched over the park, it seemed as if it were on the verge of tumbling into the wading pool below. But there was one difference— a For Sale sign sprouted out of the dead earth that served as a postage-stamp-sized front yard. How Warren could ever hope to unload that slag heap of a house was beyond me.

At one time Warren had been quite the entrepreneur, owning half a dozen decrepit houses here and there in the Annex, Seaton Village, and Little Portugal, all very central, all very desirable given the right touch. Warren's intention, during a particularly intense real estate boom a few years before, had been to fix up his seedy acquisitions and sell them quickly for a tidy profit. But Warren, whose mind may have been permanently pickled by his years of drugging in Vancouver, never quite had the knack for high-rolling speculation.

Warren's forte was the two-bit scam. He was quite adept at milking money out of the most unlikely sources. The last I'd heard he had at least a half-dozen foster children, whom some agency or other paid him reasonable amounts of money to care for. Actually, his wife, a good-natured, big-hearted, roly-poly half-Haida with some money, took care of the children, many of whom Warren employed in his shady undertakings. Warren's wife, Audrey, didn't fit the man's image: fair-haired, slim, a slick smile on his baby-fat face, Warren had his left hand on every passing woman's ass and his right in her escort's pocket. Oddly enough, Warren's father was the editor of a major Protestant denomination's weekly newspaper. Or maybe that wasn't so odd.

Warren knew everything there was to know about building liens, small claims court, mortgage juggling, and debt shirking. He was particularly crafty doing the latter. Since his properties had a dependable turnover in tenants, he simply put things like heating oil, electricity, and water in the name of long-departed lodgers. It always amazed me how long he could stall just about everybody. Of course, living in one of Warren's places meant daily visits from building code, fire, health, and heating inspectors, not to mention bailiffs, summons servers, and the police.

On the credit side, Warren did play a mean blues harp. More than once, before I came to despise him, we'd hoisted a brace of beers at a local pub that specialized in live rhythm and blues. And despite his seemingly bottomless passion for money-making schemes, Warren was a soft touch when it came to rent. Since he tended to attract less fortunate souls of like minds and personalities as denizens of his real estate, he was forever being taken to the cleaners. And, hell, he really did love his kids, even if it was in an absentminded kind of way.

Such was the make-up of Warren Crane, a man acutely skilled at inept evil in a small arena. I'm sure Warren would sell his wife if he could, but he'd probably get a bum price for her.

As I leaned against a tree, watching the house, I fancied the building changing into Warren's smooth-cheeked face with its Errol Flynn moustache, ogling the occasional female passerby. I didn't want to get any closer to the place after that hallucination, but this was where I had met Carole, and I knew I should at least see if any of the old tenants still lived there and if they, or Warren, could give me a lead on Carole's whereabouts. So I crossed the street, climbed the bombed-out steps, slipped through Warren's colossal, leering lips, and ran headlong into the real thing as he came out of the door as if shot by a cannon.

"Mickey!" he cried. "Jesus, Mickey! What are you doing here?"

I blinked, still trying to get over the feeling of being a prisoner of Warren's over-salivating mouth. "Uh, it's you."

"Jesus, Mickey, Jesus," Warren bubbled. "It's been... Jesus..."

Looking closely at Warren's piggy eyes, I thought I could detect the effects of a litre or two of Southern Comfort— his favourite drink— and several tokes. As usual he was wearing a jaunty beige tweed cap, the kind rural Irishmen are supposedly attached to. A pair of expensive-looking gun-metal wool trousers, a baggy green sweater with pandas frolicking on it, and a pair of brown penny loafers completed his wardrobe for the day.

"Warren," I said, "you're just the man I'm looking for. Have you got a moment?"

"Sure, Mickey. You want a beer? Take a seat. I'll be right back."

He went into the dark house— no electricity again? I wondered— and I sat down on the porch swing. Absently I looked out at the park next door. A bunch of kids were playing soccer, not surprising in a neighbourhood containing large numbers of Italians. Some others were playing scrub baseball on a diamond in another corner of the park, prompting me to wonder for a moment how the Blue Jays were doing in the playoffs. Or had the World Series already started? As I pondered that, one of the kids cracked a long hit right into the middle of the soccer game. A future Hank Aaron or Reggie Jackson, no doubt. Baseball always reminded me of my own childhood, days when there weren't any major-league teams in Canada and the heroes were Mickey Mantle, Willie Mays, Ernie Banks, Al Kaline, Willie McCovey, and pitching whizzes like Sandy Koufax and Whitey Ford, days when it seemed I played pick-up baseball morning, noon, and night during the short hot summers and dreamed of brand-new hockey sticks and skates when I wasn't playing shinny on the Rideau Canal in Ottawa during the dark cold winters.

It was quite the idyllic scene, the park across from Warren's, surrounded as it was on three sides by big old maples mostly stripped of leaves, their thick black branches etched on the slate sky as if by some celestial member of the Group of Seven. The day was harsher and cooler than the previous one, the annual tug of war between seasonal extremes that always had the same cruel winner.

See there, I thought. Do you see them? Trees, I answered myself. Sure, I see trees. But do you see *them,* really see *them*? Sure, I muttered in reply. Trees. They'll probably be dead in a few years. And for a moment I thought Carole was on the porch with me again, frowning and biting her lower lip at my obtuseness, my inability to see *it,* the only it that mattered. Yeah, *it,* I thought, picturing a bloated blue corpse on a cold white beach, iron-grey waves lapping at its swollen toes.

When Warren returned, he had two Labatt Blues in his hands. And I was in luck. As an added bonus, Brent Stone, one of my former fellow inmates, trailed behind him. Wearing a dirty white sailing cap, a green-striped white cotton jersey, paint-smeared white bermudas, no socks, and battered white sneakers, the blond Brent, as usual, looked as if he were about to embark on a sailing junket.

"Long time, no see," the lanky sailor said as he leaned against the porch railing and took a swig of his beer— something called Klondike Gold.

"Yeah, I guess it has," I said as Warren handed me one of the Blues and sat down beside me on the swing. "Thanks," I told Warren.

"Jesus, just like old times," Warren enthused.

Just like Falstaff and Shallow in *Henry IV,* I thought. Old buddies. Yeah, sure, we'd heard the chimes at midnight, all right. All we needed now was a roaring fire and some haunches of venison. "Where do you get Klondike Gold in Toronto?" I asked Brent. Might as well be sociable.

"Friend from B.C. drops in occasionally and brings me a case or two. Why, you want one?"

"No thanks. Just curious."

Warren was busy rolling a joint, his head bent in deep concentration as if pondering the inscrutable. I took a swig of beer. "So what are you up to these days, Brent? I didn't think you'd still be living here."

"I won't be next week. Movin' back to B.C. Actually, I moved out months ago, then moved back in three weeks ago. Warren sold the house."

"He did?" I looked at Warren. He had finished rolling the joint and was now attempting to light it.

"I shit you not," Brent said solemnly, the bottle of Klondike Gold pressed against his heart as he belched. "Fuck, I needed that. Oo-ee!" And he belched again, a long, drawn-out one this time.

"How come the For Sale sign's still up, then?" I asked.

"Fuck!" Warren said, coughing. He had just taken a massive drag on the joint. "Forgot all about it. Gotta take it down. Here," he said, extending the joint to me.

"No thanks," I said.

Warren shrugged and passed the joint to Brent, who sucked on it until I thought his lightly freckled cheeks would collapse.

"Man, that's too fine," Brent rasped when he finally exhaled.

I was always breaking the circle when pot was passed around, not so much because I didn't want to indulge, because I sometimes did, but because I didn't want to be included in the rite, didn't desire to be part of the circle. Besides, coke was more the thing these days, wasn't it? Or was it passé, too? Just then all three of us heard the mighty crack of wood against horsehide. The junior Hank Aaron had hit another monster— maybe this time all the way over to Harbord Street.

"Those Blue Jays are really something," I said inanely. When all else fails in Canada, talk about sports or the weather. "Bet they're going to take the Orioles, eh?"

"Man, where've you been?" Brent asked, flicking some ash off the joint. "The Jays got iced by Seattle last week. Four straight. The Mariners are waitin' around until either the Braves or the Giants win the NL pennant. Then it's World Series time. Oo-ee!" He knocked back some more beer, then scratched his crotch. "You know what, Mickey? Got me a boat. Yessir, a dandy sailboat waitin' for me on the coast at an ol' buddy's shack on a cove surrounded by Douglas fir. Oo-ee! I'm flyin' out next week. Hot shit!" In his own inimitable way, Brent clamped one hand in an armpit and squeezed out a resounding fake burp. "First thing I'm goin' do is buzz around the islands. Look up some chicks I know on Gabriola. Oo-ee!"

"Still going to sail around the world?" I asked.

"You bet. Not in this baby, though. My buddy's got me a job paintin' and fixin' up yachts in Vancouver. Intend to save me up a bundle an' go for it. Yessir, buy me a *real* boat!"

"Seen much of Iggy lately?" I asked.

"Iggy Klein? Shit, he's in Downsview, Etobibog, or maybe Scarberia. Ol' Iggy's walkin' the straight and narrow, ain't he, Warren?"

"Jesus, Mickey, Iggy's sellin' life insurance. Jesus!" Warren agreed, as if telling me Iggy had taken out an option on the moon and had started selling real estate there.

"Yeah, and get this," Brent added, "he bought a quarter interest in a funeral parlour out in the 'burbs somewhere. Fuck, what a guy!"

"All he needs now is to buy a store selling maternity dresses," I said, grinning like an idiot as I guzzled some more beer. We were good ol' boys jus' havin' us a fine an' dandy time, yessiree Bob.

"So where you been keepin' yourself, Mickey?" Brent asked.

"Oh, I don't live too far from here."

"Still in Seaton Village?" Warren asked.

"Yeah."

"Warren here's president of the Seaton Village Residents' Association," Brent informed me. "An' he's vice-president of the Annex Landlords' Committee. Quite the man in the community, aren't ya, Warren?"

Yeah, I thought. He'll be premier of the province next. Then I remembered that once upon a time Warren did have some naive political aspirations.

"Jesus, Mickey, you wan' another beer?" Warren asked, then checked his watch. "Shit, Audrey! I gotta get goin'. I was sup'osed to be home an hour ago. Audrey'll kill me." He winked. "Wan' another beer, Mickey?"

"No thanks, Warren. Actually, I did want to ask you if you knew anything about Carole Rutland. Remember her?"

Warren leered. "Hot stuff. How could I forget? Screwy, though. Jesus..." He drifted off, as if recalling fond physical memories of Carole.

I snapped my fingers. "Do you know where she went after you turfed her out, Warren?"

"Jesus, Mickey, I had to. She'd have burnt this house down. Fuck, she was crazy." He shook his head so hard he almost knocked his tweed cap off. "You said so yourself."

"Warren, try to think. Did she leave an address?"

"Sure, but that was over a year ago. I helped her move into a swanky place out in the Beaches. But she was only there a couple of weeks."

"How do you know that?"

"I went out to see if I could collect some of the rent she owed me. But she'd been kicked out of there, too. Bounced a rent cheque."

"Was there a forwarding address?"

"Nope. What's the matter, Mickey? She owe you money?"

"Nothing like that. What was the address in the Beaches? Do you remember?"

"Are you kiddin'?" Brent broke in. "Warren's havin' a hard time rememberin' where his houses are located, the ones he's got left, that is."

Snorting in what I assumed was a good-natured laugh, Warren drained the rest of his beer and got unsteadily to his feet. "Gotta go, guys. Audrey'll kill me." He staggered down the minefield of the steps and wobbled over to his midnight-blue 1963 Cadillac, which was parked on the street, half up on the curb. Before climbing in, he waved at us, then reached into the car, scooped up a handful of foam coffee cups and Big Mac holders, and dumped them onto the sidewalk. His cleaning chores completed, he got into the car, started the hesitant engine, and chugged away. The Cadillac resembled a drunken dinosaur on its last legs as it lurched around a corner.

"He shouldn't be driving," I said.

"Ah, you know Warren," Brent said. "He'll be okay an', anyway, that tank he drives can't go very fast. Say, by the way, about Carole Rutland. I saw her just the other day."

"What?"

"Well," he said, taking off his sailing cap, scratching his blond head, and squinting, "it was a month ago or so. The Ex was on, so it was late in August."

"That's the other day?" I said, disappointed.

"Well, sort of. Anyway, I was walkin' down Bloor not far from here, over near Honest Ed's, an' I was waitin' for the light to change, when she says, 'Hello, Brent.' I turned around, an' there she was, lookin' a little pale and scrawny, her eyes as snaky as ever. She asked me if I'd go an' have a coffee with her. Well, I wasn't sure who she was at first, then I latched on. She asked me again, an' I thought, fuck, maybe I was into somethin'. But, shit, I had to go down to the Ex. I was workin' at a water show down there an' I was already late."

"Did you get an address?" I asked impatiently.

Brent narrowed his pale blue eyes at me. "You know, I bet we'd have had us a nice little fuck if I hadn't had that job to do. She looked like she could use one, too."

I felt myself getting angry. Brent always had been an asshole, and now I was beginning to feel as if his shit were cleaving to me. "Did you get an address?"

"Real stupid of me, wasn't it? Nope, I didn't. I said somethin' like, 'Sorry, but I gotta go to work,' an' the next thing I knew she was gone. Like she'd never been there in the first place."

"Did she say anything else?"

"Not that I recall." He looked at me suspiciously. "Man, why are you so keen on findin' her? Fuck, Warren tossed her outta this place at least a year an' a half ago."

"I'm... I'm a curious kind of guy, that's all."

"Hi, there, Herbie," Brent suddenly said.

I turned around and saw Herbert Sutcliffe, big as life in a red plaid flannel shirt buttoned up to the neck and a pair of stiff new blue jeans. He was standing on the steps, glowering at us. The sight of that broad, bumpy head with its thinning shock of rust-brown hair, bulbous nose, fleshy red lips, and skewed eyes swimming behind thick bifocals sent my mind reeling back to those terrible days and nights. The gang's all here, I thought idiotically. Except for Carole. As I stared, Herbert harrumphed and tromped into the house.

"I thought he'd be long gone," I said to Brent.

"Me, too. Course, he's gotta move next week now that the dump's been sold. I tell you, Mickey, that guy gives me the fuckin' creeps. He was an unsociable bastard when you were livin' here but, fuck, he's a regular Charlie Manson these days."

"Or Jack the Ripper," I said, still shuddering at the sudden apparition of Herbert Sutcliffe.

"Well, I gotta go," Brent said, straightening. "Nice seein' you, Mickey."

"Mind if I use your can?"

"Sure, go ahead. Door's always unlocked. Nothin' to steal nowadays with just Herbie an' me. Walk right in. I gotta go down to the marina. Course, maybe you don't wanna be in that house all by your lonesome with ol' Herbie." Brent grinned, then bounded down the steps and loped toward Bloor Street at a brisk pace.

Steeling myself, I went into the house, and with some trepidation, climbed the dust-choked staircase, stopping halfway up on the landing, to look at the grimy stained-glass window of an owl tearing a mouse apart. The bathroom, the bathtub and toilet in separate rooms, was at the top of the staircase, and after I did my business in the coffin-like water closet, I lingered at the open door of my old room. Standing at the big picture window was the great unkempt bulk of Herbert Sutcliffe. He had his hamhock hands clasped tightly behind his broad back. Even from where I stood I could see he was chafing them as if agitated. I took up sentry in a dark corner of the floor where I had a good view of him but he wouldn't be able to see me.

Herbert Sutcliffe, I thought. Once, when I was living in this pleasure palace, I came home to find Herbert in the dining room— a misnomer, if ever there was one, for such a wreck of a room. He had the wobbly trestle table some of the denizens of the house ate off covered with sheets of paper. Curious, I went over to see what he was up to. He was filling in a questionnaire— hundreds of questions with multiple-choice answers, questions like "When you are suddenly woken up in the morning by the deafening sound of a jackhammer, what is your reaction? (a) panic, (b) intense anger, (c) hatred, (d) fear, (e) mild irritation, (f) indifference." Herbert had checked off (f).

Sure, I'd thought at the time. Herbert was more likely to go out and jam the jackhammer up the guy's ass, or more probably, crawl into a corner and whimper. I later learned that Herbert was always filling out behavioural tests, perhaps a legacy from his days at the Queen Street Mental Centre. I imagine he lied on every one of them.

Herbert's "girlfriend" back then gave all kinds of valuable insights into the man's wonderful nature. She was a slovenly, lumpish blind woman with buck teeth who cadged a few dollars here and there as an occasional blues singer in the city's seediest lounges, places where the greatest challenge came from the foul-mouthed, drunken mob that served as patrons and the back-up band was an ever-malfunctioning tape deck. Herbert brought her home one day and added yet another ingredient to the jolly jambalaya of that house.

Sometimes he'd leave her all alone in his room when he went out to drive his taxi, pimp, or whatever it was he did for a living. She'd start singing in a pure, sweet tremolo after a while, a mournful, plaintive blues number that would go on and on until the words dropped away and all one could hear was a continuous wail that eventually drove me out into the night.

The woman had a brother, also blind and even lumpier than she, and when the three of them got together, they'd sit in the ruin of our dining room, water dripping from a busted pipe overhead, and drink gin until they passed out. Before that, however, they'd have a merry old time. The brother played harmonica after a fashion, and he'd accompany his sister in one rollicking rhythm and blues number after another, while Herbert, wearing a party hat, would sit, hands folded in his lap, a cheesy smirk on his chalky face, in silent contemplation, as if he were in attendance at Roy Thomson Hall and Itzhak Perlman were playing violin. Welcome to year-round Hallowe'en at Warren Crane's re-creation of a Roger Corman low-budget celluloid nightmare.

One time, when Herbert had left his girlfriend behind, she confided in me that he was a bull in bed and that he had raped her the first time they'd met. Sitting there, looking into her sightless, putty-like blob of a face, I tried to imagine the two of them in bed. It was impossible. Finally, though, Herbert left her alone in the house one time too many, and she called a cab and left, never to be seen again.

Another image of Herbert that stuck in my mind was the afternoon I'd found him peeling potatoes at the dining-room table. He'd already peeled a bucket of the things with a wicked-looking, curved knife. I asked him why the hell he was paring so many spuds, since he had enough to feed a platoon by then. He told me it was therapy. His doctor had told him it was better to skin potatoes than to... Herbie never did finish the sentence. He just glared at me and continued denuding potatoes.

Lost in thought, I almost missed Herbert leaving my old room and thumping up the stairs to his own room on the third floor. He brushed by without noticing me, and I breathed a sigh of relief when I heard him close the door to his room.

Leaving the shadows, I walked into my old room. I had to look out the window to see what Herbert had been staring at so intently. Being in that room again, now bare and musty, my footfalls echoing on the scarred hardwood floor even as I tried to tiptoe, my heart struggled in my chest like a rabbit in a burlap sack. I'd spent some of the worst times of my life in this room, and here I was again.

Several dark green garbage bags stuffed with debris huddled like plump gnomes along one cracked wall. Overhead the plaster ceiling was even more water-stained than when I had stared up at it night after night, imagining it to be the lid of my coffin. But it was the window that I was interested in. For days on end I had stared out that window like a convict peering out of his cell. My window on the world. From here I'd watched the park— kids playing, couples strolling, birds twittering, squirrels fighting, leaves scattering, rain falling, my life draining away.

Now the kids I'd seen earlier in the park were gone. But I could see what had probably caught Herbert's eye. Under the maple beneath the window a man and a woman were petting quite energetically. I wondered if Herbert was still watching the couple from his own small window on the third floor, getting a different angle, so to speak. From here I could see their heads but not their hands, and judging from their spastic wriggling, their hands were quite active.

The sky had darkened the way it does sometimes on a late afternoon in the fall. It had a cold, bruised look to it, like that of a long-submerged, recently surfaced cadaver. I was getting nowhere. I wasn't any closer to Carole Rutland than when I'd started, though at least I knew she'd been around in late August. Temporally she was getting closer, if not spatially. But so what?

My eyes left the couple wrestling on the grass below and roamed to the horizon where, as always, the CN Tower blinked on and off, a concrete spear slicing through the dead flesh of the sky. I'd forgotten that all of those nights I'd spent in this room the Tower had been my constant companion. But that wasn't what was really on my mind at the moment. No, what really bothered me was that, somehow, I knew time was running out.

STATION VII

"I thought you said this place was called the Hole-in-the-Wall," I grumbled at Jerry Bauch.

"That's what I call it. Seems to fit, don't you think?" Jerry replied, the trace of a smile on his large lips, though the upturn of his mouth might have been the result of a gastric explosion in his ever-troublesome stomach.

"Sure, but you could have told me I was looking for the Paradise. I must have been in more than a dozen dumps before I found this one."

"You're here, aren't you?"

I took a gulp of my Molson Export draft beer and surveyed the large dim room. On a low stage in front of us a chubby stripper with a hard face shuffled listlessly to the bouncy beat of Madonna's "Who's That Girl?" Around us a few sullen men sat hunched over beers, their rheumy eyes following the jounce of the stripper's substantial breasts.

"Only you could find a place like this on Queen West," I said.

"This is my idea of the Queen strip, but I suppose you'd prefer the Rivoli or the Queen Mother."

"Spare me the puns, Jerry."

He gave me another dyspeptic smile. "I hate to leave when Pepper Lane's starting to get into gear, but I had at least two beers before you finally arrived." He pushed back his chair and made his way toward the basement washroom.

Watching Jerry's pear-shaped bulk wobble off, I fancied him a latter-day Samuel Johnson, or perhaps Balzac. Actually, as far as his face went, Jerry reminded me of busts I'd seen of the Roman emperors Vitellius and Vespasian. All he needed was a toga. With his great head, generous nose, fleshy lips, double chin, and massive neck, Jerry seemed a figure from another age, incongruously garbed in a tent-like silk shirt decorated with tiny copulating couples—Jerry's walking advertisement for the *Kama Sutra*—and a pair of stiff new blue jeans that looked as if they'd easily accommodate several people if they weren't already occupied by Jerry's considerable thighs. Scuffed black oxfords completed Jerry's outfit for the night, testifying to his wondrous ability to favour fashion no other journalist under sixty would ever contemplate.

Jerry enjoyed being out of step with his era. He revelled in the role of caustic cynic, and his heroes tended to be writers like Aristophanes, Jonathan Swift, Samuel Johnson, Oscar Wilde, and Henri de Montherlant. Among his favourite fictional heroes were the Vicomte de Valmont, the master seducer of *Les Liaisons Dangereuses*; Balzac's satanic Vautrin; the devious Chichikov in Gogol's *Dead Souls*; the hedonistic corruptor, Sir Henry Wotton, in Wilde's *The Picture of Dorian Gray*; and Walter Burns, the hard-bitten newspaper editor of *The Front Page*. Of course, inevitably, two of his best-loved actors were the young, misogynistic Robert Ryan in Fritz Lang's *Clash by Night,* and the ever-sneering George Sanders in just about anything.

Given Jerry's frequently virulent homophobia, the sexual inclination of many of his cherished putdown artists must have caused him some distress, though Jerry tended to ignore that side of his heroes even as he flailed the likes of André Gide, Jean Cocteau, Christopher Isherwood, E.M. Forster, and Gore Vidal, et al., principally because of their sexual persuasion. As Jerry put it, "There are good artists, there are bad artists, and there are homo artists." But writers such as Marcel Proust, in Jerry's view, were exempt from the paradigm. When Jerry admired someone, homosexuality didn't matter any more, and Jerry must have admired Proust— he'd spent the past few years labouring to read *Remembrance of Things Past* in the original French. As for Jerry's own sexuality, the writer who came to mind when drawing parallels had to be randy old Samuel Pepys. I often wondered if Jerry, too, kept a diary, recording everything from frequency of masturbation to the position used with his latest feminine conquest. Big as Jerry was, he did seem to have a way with women.

One of the many things that mystified me about Jerry, though, was the fact that he resided in Cabbagetown, just a stone's throw from Allan Gardens. Here one found the city's greatest concentration of gays, not to mention a curious smorgasbord of post-yuppies, white trash, pimps, hookers, street kids, rummies, and the sensationally insane. Jerry seemed to hate every last resident of his neighbourhood, but he wouldn't think of living anywhere else.

A low murmur had risen in the room, and I glanced at the stage to see what the excitement was about. Pepper Lane had peeled off her G-string, and except for her hand-tooled cowboy boots, was stark naked. That wasn't the cause of the hubbub, though— Pepper's ample blue-grey flesh wouldn't arouse a pack of sewer rats. No, the excitement was due to Pepper's unique talent for picking up five-dollar bills with her vaginal lips. A couple of fascinated drunks were trying to find out if Pepper could also quaff beer with the wondrous appendage. Ever accommodating, Pepper squatted over a beer glass and accomplished the miracle to a round of applause.

"She should have her own TV show," Jerry suggested as he sat down at our table.

"Remarkable," I agreed.

Jerry drained the remainder of his beer, then said, "I vote we have another round. It's been a while since we got together like this."

"It hasn't been that long, really. A month. Maybe two. I'll admit, though, it seems like I've spent the past two years in solitary confinement."

"You've got friends, or do you think of nights like this as visiting hours?"

"Yeah, I've got friends— *a* friend." I looked at Jerry and tried to grin.

"What about that professor? Which reminds me. Isn't that the reason for this meeting? You were supposed to get me some leads on *Cardenio* and its ever-buggering mystery."

I winced. "No dice, Jerry. I couldn't get hold of Jack. Believe me, I tried."

"Shit!" He gave me a withering look and ordered another round of beer from the anorexic blonde waitress who tramped wraith-like between tables, a king-sized cigarette dangling from her dead-fish lower lip.

"Now what were you saying about getting together with friends for the sake of getting together?"

"Damn it, Mickey, I'm not getting anywhere with this *Cardenio* business."

"Have you talked with Kaplan, the cop investigating the theft?"

"Of course, but he's not much further ahead than I am."

"He's been checking out antiquarian shops, you know."

"So? That's routine."

"Well, this might interest you. I happened to have business at a shop called Vathek, down the street. It's a real charmer of a store that sells everything from nail-studded dildoes to exquisite nineteenth-century Japanese woodcuts. Anyway, I ran into Nik Rorke there. It seems he works for the owner, Cedric Shaw."

Jerry's left eyebrow curled upward. George Sanders as Samuel Johnson, or maybe Rush Limbaugh. I wasn't sure what had sparked his interest, though— the dildoes or Nik Rorke. "Really?" he said.

"And get this, there's a character named Donald Yates also working for Shaw. He's the guy I was paying a visit."

"Whoa, slow down. You've lost me. Why were you, as you put it, 'paying a visit' to this Mr. Yates?"

"That's right, I haven't told you yet. I've been trying to find a woman named Carole Rutland."

This time both eyebrows curled. "Let me see, you used to be a reporter. Have I missed something? Did you get a new job? Let me guess. You're working for the RCMP—"

"Fuck, Jerry, let me finish, will you?"

"Nice mouth. Talk to your mother that way?"

"I don't have a mother," I said irritably.

"Now we get to the root of the problem."

"You're a born sneerer, Jerry."

"And you're not?"

I thought about that for a moment.

"Who's infecting whom?" Jerry added.

"Maybe we keep each other on our toes."

"Yeah, you do wonders for my self-esteem."

I was startled. Jerry seldom let down his guard. "Enough self-analysis. Can I finish my story?"

"Please. I'm entranced."

"Last week I got a call for Carole Rutland and, well, it triggered my curiosity. The caller hung up before I could find out who it was."

"I take it you know this Carole Rutland?"

"I used to share a house with her. I thought I'd see if I could find out where she is and how she's doing."

"Why?"

There was that question again— why? "Shit, I don't know. No special reason."

Jerry shook his large head, then took his horn-rimmed glasses from his shirt pocket, put them on, and peered at me.

"Cut it out, Jerry," I said, pushing his face away.

He sat back in his chair. "You never learn, do you?"

"What do you mean?"

"I bet you read every child's version of the exploits of King Arthur and his chivalric comrades that you could get your sweaty little nine-year-old hands on."

"Listen, I'm... worried about her. I have a feeling something's wrong."

This brought a smile of approval to Jerry's face. "Oh, well, that's different. It's about time you had a healthy interest in another woman."

"It's not like that. I mean, shit, I didn't even really like Carole. I mean, she was damn attractive, but she's nuts."

Jerry frowned, then looked around the room. Pepper Lane, taking a break, was sitting with two men and a woman at a table over in one corner. Golden oldies from the sixties gurgled from the speakers. "That's the owner of this joint," he finally said. "See the dumpy peroxide blonde with a face like the floor of the men's room at a Salvation Army hostel? Her name's Bert. She used to be married to a guy who rode with Satan's Choice. Has the tattoos to prove it. You know, you might try saving her."

"I knew this had a point somewhere," I snapped. "The reason I'm telling you about Carole is because one of her friends— Sharon Praeger— was murdered the other day."

"That house you used to share was filled with crazies, wasn't it?"

"Yeah."

"Well, a murder shouldn't seem all that out of place."

"Sharon must have been killed shortly after I saw her. She's the one who told me about Yates, the guy at Vathek."

"Hmm. So you think Praeger's murder... Wait a minute. She's the one who was hammered to death like all those others. What are you talking about here, your disappearing friend or a serial killer? Where does *Cardenio* fit into all of this?"

"I'm not saying it does."

"You think your nutty Andromeda got bopped by this guy who's butchering all those other women?"

"That's what Kaplan asked me, more or less. He says they haven't linked Praeger's murder with the others yet."

"So what are you trying to say?"

"Maybe someone's taking advantage of the serial killings. You know, one more won't hurt and who's to know. The real psycho sure won't object."

"Ah, I get it now. 'What's in a name? That which we call a hammer, by any other name would pulverize as well.'"

"You do know how to turn a phrase."

"So now you've got two damsels— a dead one and a gone one. I'm happy for you, Mickey. You have your own nice little mystery, but it's not helping me with *Cardenio*."

"There's Nik Rorke, don't forget."

"Let's see, the last time I heard, ol' Nik wasn't into literary pursuits."

"No, but Cedric Shaw is."

"Ah, the connection! Didn't Rorke have something to do with Al Karp, the alderman for Ward Two back when you were still a knight in elbow-patched tweed riding through the wastelands of political chicanery?"

I stared at Jerry and took a long swig of beer. "Yeah."

"And wasn't it alleged that Nik Rorke dug up all that dirt on Diane Davis, the lady who ran for mayor against Karp?"

I could feel myself getting numb.

"And didn't a youngish reporter who probably watched too many hours of Watergate hearings when he was a wee lad swallow all that dirt which, by the way, was true? And didn't his newspaper run a series of sensational articles that made this earnest young man the talk of the town?"

I gripped my empty beer glass with a hand that no longer felt attached to me.

"And didn't the object of this prize-winning reportage, the aforementioned Ms. Davis, jump to her death from one of our fair city's lofty bank towers?"

"Are you finished?" I managed to squeeze out.

"You're always letting yourself get fucked up and fucked by women, Mickey. If it isn't that pathetic Diane Davis, who did, as you well know, fuck the teenaged girls in the battered kids' refuge she ran, it's a stray looney like this Carole Rutland broad, or even a corpse, for Christ's sake, or even better, your darling former—"

"I said, are you finished?"

"Yes, I'm finished."

Rather than talk any more, we nursed another round of beer. A new stripper had taken the stage— a glistening black butterball— and Jerry gave her his full attention. I sat there and thought about things I tried not to think about these days. Things like Diane Davis.

Sure, maybe she did do everything my articles accused her of, but did I have to write about them? Oh, yeah, I'd told myself someone else would if I hadn't. And there was the fame. With the Davis articles I'd really begun to make a name for myself. After she jumped, well, if I'd been someone else with a thicker skin, I'd have merely gone on to tackle, say, Al Karp, the man I should have been exposing in the first place. That might have been one way to make amends. Instead, I folded like a tent and went down the tubes.

Someone did get Karp in the end, though. As he was walking to his car just a few days before the election, a young girl stepped out of the bushes and emptied a .22 into his face. After the murder, an enterprising reporter dug up all kinds of slime that Karp had had his fingers in. It made me sick to know that, had Karp lived, he would almost certainly have been elected mayor.

Good reasons for a slide? I'd thought so, I guess, but Laura hadn't. I'm not sure if she began to despise me because of my role in the Davis affair or because I let it get to me so much that I rolled over and played dead. She wanted me to be a success even more than I did, and after Davis, thought I should go after Karp before someone else did. Time and again she'd tell me that I wasn't responsible for Davis's death. But she could never convince me. I looked into the Davis affair a lot deeper after her suicide, and though it was true she had a thing for young girls, she wasn't a bad person. The young girl who blew away Karp had been one of Ms. Davis's teenaged lovers.

The whole business made me sick to death. What was right? What was good? Bad? Moral? I didn't know any more, wasn't sure if I'd ever known. All I wanted was to wash my hands of it and get out. Or was that really the truth? Karp scared me, and Rorke even more. I never could put my finger on just what my reasons were for quitting my job at the *Globe*. And if I couldn't get a handle on the mess, how could I expect Laura to?

As I slid deeper into my own moral quagmire, Laura drifted farther away. She was a dental hygienist who thought I was going to be world-famous some day. That was part of whatever attraction I had for her. And when I threw in the towel, she tried to understand— I'll give her that— but, well, one day she was cleaning the teeth of a new patient, a corporate lawyer with shaggy black hair and beard, and that was that.

Now she's living on Vancouver Island with her shaggy lover. Even has a kid, I hear. A boy. I'd always wanted kids with Laura. Even before the Davis affair, that had been one of our problems— her reluctance to have kids. Part of her lack of certainty about me, no doubt.

I think she lives in Sooke in order to get as far away from me as possible without leaving the country. Laura blamed me for messing up her life, as if I were a lost investment on the emotional exchange, maybe even the financial one. Nah, that was a cheap shot. It wasn't just that. There was guilt mixed in there somewhere with the contempt, hatred, resentment, and love. Yeah, love. I think she needed the distance because she still loved me, after a fashion, and she didn't want a box seat on the wreck I'd become, nor did she want too close a reminder of her own behaviour. But I guess it didn't matter what Laura thought, believed, or felt. I could only guess at stuff like that, but I knew with dead certainty that I was still in love with her despite everything. And despite what well-meaning people kept telling me, the sting wasn't getting any less painful. The only difference now was that I was less dependent on booze to anesthetize the wound. These days I was pretty good at packing my soul with psychological dry ice.

"You're missing all the fun," Jerry suddenly said to me, breaking into my rigorous self-examination.

I glanced at the stage. The beefy black woman was down to her G-string, which the appreciative audience had stuffed five-dollar bills into. She had water pistols in both of her pudgy hands and was zapping the zombies in the bar with great glee when she wasn't making obscene gestures with the toy guns— all of this to the accompaniment of Carlos Santana's version of "Black Magic."

"I see what you mean," I said.

"Are you okay?"

"Yeah, sure, Jerry. I was just taking a trip down memory lane. You play pretty tough hardball, you know."

"You worry me, Mickey."

"I've got to find Carole Rutland, Jerry."

"Why?"

"Something's rotten. I know it. And I've got to follow it until the end. No more hiding under the covers."

"Even if Nik Rorke's under the bed?"

"Even if Nik Rorke's in the bed."

"They say he crippled that reporter who dug into the Karp business after the honourable alderman's untimely demise."

"They couldn't prove it."

"No one ever does with Rorke."

"The Big Bad Wolf."

"Rorke?"

"No, I mean that guy sitting over in the corner with Pepper Lane. I just noticed him."

Jerry squinted. "You mean the big guy in the red plaid hunting vest?"

"Yeah, him, Herbert Sutcliffe. I wonder what he's doing here."

"Same as everyone else, I imagine."

"He seems to know Pepper."

"Maybe they have professional dealings. Pepper has her vaginal lips dipped into other activities, you know."

"I'd always thought he pimped or something. Wait, he's getting up."

We both watched as Herbert lumbered toward the door.

"Going for his evening constitutional perhaps," Jerry said, sipping from his beer. "Why are you so interested in this guy?"

"I'm beginning to think he's part of the equation. Listen, I'm going to follow him and see what he's up to."

"There you go playing cop again."

"Come on, we'd better hustle or he'll get away."

Jerry glared at me with disbelief. "I intend to continue sitting right where

I am watching the finest Queen Street West has to offer parading their fleshly delights in front of my jaded eyes. Besides, I don't even know why you want to chase—"

But I was already halfway to the door, saying, "Call you later."

STATION VIII

Outside on Queen Street I looked frantically around for Herbert. I wasn't really sure why I had to follow him, but I knew I'd be disappointed if I lost him. Luck was with me, though, because he wasn't driving his cab tonight. Instead he was standing at the westbound streetcar stop opposite the Paradise. There was a sizable group of people waiting with him, which I joined, hanging around its edges and out of sight.

Looming above us out of the gloom of a crisp, cold night was the monolithic CN Tower, a red-and-blue rocket about to take off. And as I studied the Tower, another rocket, this one an old red-and-yellow streetcar, ground to a metal-crunching halt in front of us. Herbert glanced furtively around, then climbed on. The streetcar was packed, but I managed to find a spot where I could keep an eye on Herbert, whose bulk now occupied a seat in the rear.

We clanged and jerked our way along Queen, making frequent stops. Eventually, as the crowd thinned, I had to find a seat where I could observe Herbert yet not be noticed by him. I shouldn't have worried; the Yorkshireman spent the entire trip glaring out the window.

I had lots of time to wonder some more about following the guy. Somehow, when I'd spotted him in the Paradise, I'd known he was my best lead concerning Carole's whereabouts. The man pulsed with rage and violence. His meaty face squatted like a malignant toad over chunky shoulders swathed in red plaid. His rust-brown hair was slicked back and glistened moistly in the streetcar's harsh lighting. His bulging eyes were black-rimmed tonight, giving him the appearance of a psychotic raccoon with a thyroid problem. Maybe that's why I was following the asshole. Disgust. I *hoped* the guy was up to something.

One thing was certain: Herbert was more strung out than usual. In that hunting jacket it wasn't hard to picture him wielding an axe or a chain saw. Mumbling to myself, I peered out the window and watched the shabby parade of textile dyers, remnant shops, electrical appliance stores, scuzzy hotels, palm-reading parlours, greasy open kitchens, used furniture emporia, and ragtag restaurants of undefined ethnicity peel on by. When the Queen Street Mental Health Centre, Herbie's onetime respite from the madding crowd, came into view, I snuck a look to see if his old alma mater struck a tear. But my spying was interrupted by a blood-curdling laugh let loose by a female gargoyle sitting behind me. We had entered Parkdale, land of a hundred halfway houses, an occasion the hysterical harpy no doubt felt should be marked with appropriate melodrama.

We were pretty far out now, which started me worrying. Just where the hell was the guy going? If we kept trundling along Queen, we'd end up... But I didn't get the thought finished. Sunnyside and the Palais Royale Dance Hall flashed by and we were right up against the dark velvet lake and its asphalt-and-concrete straitjacket. I now knew where Herbie was heading— High Park, the city's biggest park.

But why? At this time of night? Was Herbie into midnight picnics? The park, perched near the old city's western extremity, was filled with trees, ponds, and rolling hills. At night it was a dark, lonely place.

Just then the streetcar came to an abrupt halt, and sure enough Herbie jumped off via the rear doors, while I exited from the front. Maybe, I thought, old Herbie has a friend out this way. Give the guy the benefit of the doubt. People lived out here, too. We weren't exactly in the wilderness, but as I cautiously slipped into the park after Herbie, I knew I might as well be entering a jungle in pursuit of a tiger, better still, a mad rhino.

Herbie was in a hurry. Despite the lumbering nature of his gait, he was keeping up a brisk pace. I had to be careful; I didn't want him to spot me.

But as we got farther into the woods there was a good chance I might lose him. For the moment, though, Herbie stuck to the shore of one of the park's willow-bordered ponds, forcing me to hang back at some distance. A sudden splash in the water spooked me. Ducks, I thought. Or maybe frogs. And then I nearly tripped over something big, something that tried to bite me. There was a whole lot of honking and hissing, and I realized I'd stumbled onto a flock of Canada geese. Probably disturbed their beauty sleep. Luckily, they were only mildly upset.

Somehow Herbie had managed to avoid the geese, but I figured all the noise I'd caused must have caught his attention, so I squatted among the unappreciative birds for a moment until the coast was clear. Around me dark lumps with long necks milled about. I felt goddamn silly, but that mood was quickly replaced by new fears of losing my after-hours date. Without further ado, I parted company with my newfound friends.

Herbie veered off the path and headed up a hill and into the trees. It didn't take me long to get claustrophobic and apprehensive amid the big oaks and maples. Every time a bird squawked or a squirrel rustled in the underbrush, I became a candidate for intensive care. Ahead of me, Herbie seemed to get bigger and bigger, his wide back tripling in size until all I could see were his heaving shoulders surmounted by a massive head. And wasn't that an axe in his right paw, after all?

Then, without warning, he whipped around. My reflexes turned out to be not that bad despite the fear clutching my every muscle. I just managed to duck behind a bush. Herbie stood there for a few seconds, and I heard his breathing, a giant bellows filling my ears, threatening to burst them. I had to look up to convince myself he wasn't towering over me and on the verge of splitting my head open as if it were a pumpkin. But he continued on his way, stepping up the pace.

I had no idea where we were at this point— somewhere in the middle of the park, no doubt. At this time of night the illusion that we were in the northern bush was all too real. I kept muttering to myself, regretting every step into the dark forest that got denser with each passing minute.

Finally Herbie stopped. He seemed to be listening to something. All I could hear was my own ragged breathing, the wind in the trees, and the rustle of leaves. Up in the sky, the moon, to my alarm, was full. At least, I thought, it provided some light, but that proved only temporary as clouds wrapped it up tight and I found myself back in the forest with an ogre a dozen or so yards away. Any moment now and I'd start hearing wolves howl. Instead I picked out what Herbie must have noticed. Someone was coming our way.

On the other side of the bushes there was a park path. I tried hard to see who the footfalls belonged to. It was too gloomy, though, and as I made up my mind to try to get closer, the moon popped out for a return engagement. Marching down the path was a woman in a yellow raincoat. Beside her was a white fluff that might have been a poodle.

I couldn't believe it! Who could be crazy enough to walk her dog in the middle of an isolated park in a city upping its quota of mass murder? Little Yellow Riding Hood and Toto. Fairy-tale ghoulash. And what was Herbie? Everybody's nightmare? Mine especially. More particularly that of the girl in the raincoat.

The guy had a record as a rapist. What the hell else would he be doing in this park ogling the dog lover? Panic sat beside me in the bush, then it jumped on me. I had to do something, but all I could do was watch. For a moment I got things confused. Here I was hunkered behind a bush in a dark park late at night, the moon full, but that was crazy, and I jerked my head toward Herbie. And this time there was something in his hand. I caught a flash of metal. A knife? A hammer?

The woman's footfalls became my heartbeat, and I tried to push myself out of the bush before Herbie sprang. But just when I thought I'd arm-wrestled panic to the ground, all hell broke lose. Herbie let out a growl that made my hair stand on end and leaped at Little Yellow Riding Hood, but as he did a squad of cops came out of nowhere and tackled him. I sagged back into the bush, my heart banging against my brain. But I didn't get much time to relax. Someone grabbed me from behind in a half-nelson and pushed me into the leaves face first.

"Don't tell me," a voice rasped in my ear. "You guys are workin' in pairs these days, right?" The guy frisked me roughly, then flipped me over. "Hey, Charlie, I got another one over here. The woods are crawlin' with creeps tonight."

My attacker was a uniformed cop imitating a brick wall. He was short and wide, had bright red hair and freckles, and was waving a gun and a powerful flashlight in my face.

"On your feet," he growled.

"Sure," I said. "No problem. See, I'm on my feet."

"Wise guy, eh?"

"Look, you've got the wrong idea."

"Yeah. Don't we always."

At that point the rest of the cops and Little Yellow Riding Hood had joined us.

"What you got?" a plainclothes cop asked. He wore a single-breasted trench coat of indeterminate colour, had no hair, and owned a face you could cut glass with.

"Another pervert in the bush," the brick wall said. "Christ, these guys bring back-up now."

Two of the uniforms had Herbie handcuffed off to one side. He'd shrunken considerably. A pint-size Grendel, to say the least. He hadn't noticed me yet; he was too busy communicating with the ground. I had a wild idea that maybe I could get Herbie to vouch for me. Something like, "Hey, yeah, I know this guy. He's just your friendly neighbourhood monster watcher."

"Hey, Sarge," another cop burst out, "look at this!"

Sarge was the bald detective in the beaten-up trench coat. The uniform held up a long steel hammer with a red leather handle. Visibility was improving every minute, what with cops tramping through the vegetation with flashlights and lanterns.

Baldy lost interest in me and went over to the uniform. "For Christ's sake, Mulroney, get your goddamn hands off it. Fuck, don't they teach you guys anything?"

Little Yellow Riding Hood was puffing on a cigarette and conferring with three of the uniforms. She looked like one of the boys. A stake-out! It had to be. The police were under the gun. Someone was hammering his way through the city's women. The less reputable types were calling him Hammer Harry. Make that Hammer Herbie. Right now the cops were as excited as kids at a fish fry. Maybe while they wrapped up their catch I could sidle off.

"Where do you think you're goin'?" the brick wall bellowed. "Hey, Sarge, what do we do with this one?"

Reluctantly Baldy came back, scowling as he manoeuvred around a horse cop. "Okay, you, let's have it. We know the other creep. Where do you come in? You two some kind of fucked-up dynamic duo?"

"Listen, Sergeant... ?"

"Craddock."

"My name's Mickey Finnegan. I... I know Ham— I know who he is, the guy you caught."

"Terrific! Now tell me something I don't know."

Craddock was all edges and sharp points, but he tried hard to pass himself off as some kind of Kojak. Cops shouldn't watch television, I thought. Or at least they should keep up with the times. Iron Johns with balls would be more apropos.

"Shit, listen, it's too hard to explain. Contact Sergeant Frank Kaplan over at 52 Division. He'll vouch for me."

"Sure." Craddock grinned at the brick wall. He grinned at Little Yellow Riding Hood. He even grinned at Herbie. "Sure." Then he spun around. "C'mon, for fuck's sake! What are we standin' around here for? Let's move! Christ, I hate trees."

At that moment I couldn't have agreed more. As Herbie and I— he still hadn't recognized me— were herded off toward the nearest parking lot, I couldn't help noticing the Tower again. Even in the forest it floated malevolently overhead.

STATION IX

Was Herbie Sutcliffe Hammer Harry? Sergeant Craddock and his merry men were certainly convinced. After Herbie's rape record and psychological profile arrived, even Herbie's mother, if he had ever had one, would have bought it.

The more I told Craddock and the boys my story, the funnier they thought it was. I'd heard horror tales about the lock-up at 52 Division, Kaplan's hang-out— everybody in Toronto had. No doubt Craddock and his minions wanted to make sure their cop shop near High Park didn't miss out on the good press.

Craddock was a lacrosse player, and he kept measuring my head with his lacrosse stick all through our friendly chat. He never hit me; he just swatted the air near my head as if protecting me from an invisible swarm of killer bees. We played good cop/bad cop. We played "You No Talk, We Leave You Alone in Big Bad Cell." We even played Trivial Pursuit. Only the trivia concerned my life and the sergeant didn't like my answers.

Finally, after hours of mental rhumba, Craddock called Kaplan, who, against his better judgement, vouched for me. It was seven in the morning by the time I was released, and all I could think of was heading home and crawling into bed, preferably with the covers over my head. I didn't want to think about Carole any more. Or Sharon Praeger. Or Laura. Or anyone. When, during a weak moment, I'd mentioned Carole to Craddock, he'd loved it. Chalk another one up for Hammer Harry. Who cares if they hadn't found the body yet. Craddock, the police chief, the mayor, the premier, they'd all be happy to dump everything from the baby killings at Sick Children's Hospital to the province's many unsolved child murders on Herbie's chunky shoulders.

As for me, I drifted zombie-like through the morning rush-hour streets of Toronto, intent on oblivion by bottle, bed, or both. When I got home, though, the fridge was bare of beer and the cupboard wanting for whiskey, so I opted for the sheets. Just as I was nicely settling down to sleep off the rest of the century, the phone rang, as it always does in such situations. I figured it would be Kaplan on a tear to chew me out, so I decided to ignore the ringing. I'd forgotten to leave my answering machine on, but I assumed the caller would give up eventually. That didn't happen, and reluctantly I picked up the receiver of the phone that I'd conveniently moved to my bedroom.

"Yeah?" I groaned.

"Finnegan? Mickey Finnegan?"

"Speaking, sort of."

"It's Donald Yates, from Vathek. Remember?"

I sat up on my futon as if I'd been slugged by Herbie's hammer. "Yates? Sure, I remember."

"Did you... did you read about Sharon in the paper the other day?"

I didn't want to talk to the guy. I didn't want to think about Vathek and Cedric Shaw and Nik Rorke. It was all over. They'd find Carole's body sooner or later. The hammer would match. I should never have gotten out from under the blankets. The blankets were my friends. My only friends.

"Mr. Finnegan? Are you there?"

"No."

"What?" The twitching rabbit on the other end of the line sounded confused. He was probably gnawing on his receiver. "I'm scared, Mr. Finnegan. I'm—"

"You're scared? What the hell is this, Yates? Do you have some goddamn compulsion to call strangers in the middle of the night and bend their ears with your anxieties?"

"It's eight-thirty in the morning, Mr. Finnegan. Hardly the middle of the night. I tried to reach you last night." Then he harrumphed. I hate harrumphers. Yates would have made a good civil servant.

"What's a nice guy like you doing in a place like Vathek?" I rasped.

"Pardon? Are you drunk, Mr. Finnegan?"

"No, but I wish I was. Get to the point, Yates. What do you want?"

He harrumphed again. "Sharon's death was no accident, you know."

"Yeah, I guessed that. Not too many hammers run people over these days. Christ, Yates, I've been jawing with cops all night and listening to drunks and dopeheads try out for the Mormon Tabernacle Choir. I want to sleep."

"I know... Sharon's death... was too close for comfort..."

"Time's up."

"No, wait, Mr. Finnegan. I know things. So did Sharon. I'm scared."

"Listen, Yates, Hammer Harry's been caught. Take it from me. I was there. And even if he hadn't been, you're not his type."

"You don't get it, do you? Carole's gone. Now Sharon. I'm next, Finnegan. I tell you, I'm next." The rabbit really was scared. He was terrified.

"Calm down."

"I... I've got to go to work. Will you meet me tonight?"

I looked up at the ceiling for a moment, then back down at my blanket. "Okay."

"There's a little café on Queen West not far from Vathek. It's called the Blue Hog. I'll meet you there after work, say, six o'clock. Okay?"

"Can't wait," I said, hanging up.

A date with Donald Yates. Wonderful, I thought, as I burrowed into the bedclothes once again. Maybe I could open up a clinic for the dispossessed and the disturbed. I was getting to be a regular Mother Teresa. With visions of hammers and hobgoblins dancing in my brain, I finally fell asleep.

Six hours or so later I woke up, thirsty as hell and ravenous. I made myself an omelette with some questionable Kraft old cheddar cheese, then went to the local beer store and bought a two-four of Molson Export. Another hour later I'd quaffed a trio of beers and was starting to feel pretty good. I decided I needed back-up for my meet with Mr. Yates and called Jerry Bauch. Telling him I might have an angle on the *Cardenio* case which, of course, I didn't, I asked him to be at the Blue Hog at six. Then I took a long, hot shower, dressed, and headed out the door. Somehow I knew I had a long way to go before I could hide under the covers again.

When I got to the Blue Hog, Jerry was already there. I wasn't noted for my punctuality, and Jerry invariably arrived before me. Tonight he was wearing his *Globe and Mail* costume— a white flannel suit and a Panama hat. Only Jerry would wear such a get-up in the fall. He looked a little like Sidney Greenstreet in *The Maltese Falcon*. Once, I called him Gutman when he was wearing the outfit. It was the first and last time. His face had stiffened, his eyes had turned into menacing slits, and his plump, moist lips had blanched, then quivered ever so slightly. He didn't talk to me for weeks after that. Only Jerry Bauch could make cracks about Jerry Bauch's girth. No one else. Period. I hate to think what he would have done if I'd mentioned Tom Wolfe, his least-favourite journalist.

Now, as I sat down on a hard little Italian bistro chair, the kind designed with torture in mind, he said, "We've got to stop meeting this way. Two nights in a row. My heart can't take the excitement."

"What are you drinking?" I asked.

"Though the mere look and name of this place make me cringe, this establishment does make a pretty mean Turkish coffee. No doubt one of the more arcane ethnic mysteries of our dear old city."

I looked around. Judging by the bar, which seemed poised to take off on an interstellar voyage, and the chairs and tables, the Blue Hog was some sort of attempt at urban Italian café chic rerouted through a southern Ontarian's idea of Manhattan mod. The joint's name was obviously thrown in for Canadian content laws and a weak attempt at local humour. A Cinzano or a glass of Chianti was probably de rigueur here, but I opted for a double rye on the rocks.

"My, my," Jerry said, "you must have worked up a thirst after your adventure last night."

"You know about it?"

"Don't you ever read the papers, Mickey? The capture of Hammer Harry, or Herbie, as the case may be, sent my fellow scribes into a newsprint frenzy of prodigious proportions. Throwing you in jolted them into alliterative apoplexy, or is that oxymoronic orgasm? You're famous, m'boy. How did one paper put it? 'Hammer Harry Mickey Finneganed.'"

"Very funny, Jerry."

"So, now that your little mystery seems to be solved, what about mine? Didn't you say you had, as you quaintly put it, a new angle on the *Cardenio* business?"

"Do you think the play's real?"

"Always answer a question with another question. That's my Mickey.

Well, as a matter of fact, I've done a little homework on the subject. There are a few records of *Cardenio*. A court performance in 1613 of the play by the King's Men, Shakespeare's theatre company. Then in 1653 a man named Humphrey Moseley, a collector of old manuscripts, attributed the play to Shakespeare and John Fletcher, the guy Shakespeare collaborated with on *The Two Noble Kinsmen* and *Henry VIII,* his last two dramas. And in the eighteenth century there was a newspaper reference to a *Cardenio* manuscript in the library of the Covent Garden Playhouse. Unfortunately the theatre burned down in 1808, and *Cardenio* disappeared from history... until now."

"I guess that means you think it does exist."

"That's not the point, is it? Someone does. Now maybe you can tell me what that new angle is."

"I don't know what I have. Like I told you, I'm meeting Yates here."

"I fail to see what he's got to do with *Cardenio*. The police can't connect Cedric Shaw or Vathek to the manuscript. This has got something to do with that girl you're looking for, hasn't it? You haven't given up on that, after all."

"Jerry, Yates is scared shitless."

"But aren't we all?"

Just then I spied His Preppiness Himself in one of the café's multitudinous mirrors. "Here he comes now," I said, downing a half inch of rye.

When Yates got to our table, he paused, a look of alarm creeping across his white-bread, blond-coiffed head. "W-who's this?" he quacked.

"A friend, Donald. Just a friend. Sit down and take a load off your heart. I'm sure it's been working double time lately."

"I said just you, Finnegan. No one else."

"Donald, it's okay, believe me. This is Jerry Bauch."

"The movie critic?"

Jerry bestowed the kind of withering smile on Yates that I imagined Nero had reserved for Christians destined to be lion lunches. "I've been known to watch a *film* or two in my time," he said.

For some reason Jerry's occupation allayed Yates's fears. Maybe he figured film critics were harmless, at least physically. "I write myself, you know," he said, his reddish nostrils twitching. "I simply adored the latest Atom Egoyan."

Yates certainly wasn't very discerning. Jerry now had murder in his eye. Mentioning Atom Egoyan positively was about the worst thing you could say to him professionally.

"Yates," I piped up, "sit down and tell me what you're so wired about."

Yates the budding film critic was replaced by Yates the terrified rabbit, but he sat down. Running his bud-like tongue over his lower lip, he said, "I... what about him?" His eyes flicked to Jerry.

"I told you, Donald, Jerry's a friend with an interest in this, particularly *Cardenio*." I didn't think it was possible, but Yates's face got even paler.

"W-who said anything about *Cardenio*?"

"No one, but my hunch is Cedric Shaw has something to do with stealing that manuscript. I'm sure he doesn't employ Nik Rorke as a bicycle courier."

"Nik Rorke?" Yates gasped. It was nice to see that I wasn't the only one adversely affected by that name.

"Okay, Donald, let's start with something simple, like Carole Rutland. What do you know?"

Yates's pinkish eyes hopped around the café, no doubt seeing Nik Rorke beneath every wrought-iron, fake marble-topped table. "We're too close."

"You picked this place, Yates, not me. Do you know where Carole is? Does Sharon's murder have something to do with her disappearance?"

"Who said she disappeared?"

"Well, if she hasn't, she's doing a pretty good imitation."

"Sharon. The papers say it was the psychopath."

"If you believed that, Mr. Yates," Jerry interjected, "we wouldn't be here now, would we?"

"I guess not," Yates agreed, then twisted his head and stared out the café window. "She used to work over there, you know,"

I looked across the street and saw a sign with a fat Buddha on a cloud. "Who?" I asked, my exasperation mounting. "Sharon?"

"No... no, Carole. Nirvana. She used to work at Nirvana. It's a centre for consciousness-raising. They sell books on yoga, Buddhism, Taoism, all kinds of Eastern mysticism. It's a restaurant, too— organic vegetarianism. And they have concerts. Lots of Ravi Shankar-type stuff."

"Figures," I said. "Sounds like Carole."

"That's where she met him."

"Met who?" Jerry exclaimed, beating me to the punch.

"Macpherson. Gavin... no, Garrett Macpherson, the U of T professor who found that manuscript."

Jerry's furled eyebrows nearly touched the ceiling. "At long last, relevance."

"So Macpherson knows Carole," I said, whistling.

Yates leaned forward. "I need a drink."

"Be my guest," I said.

The blond sales clerk ordered a strawberry daiquiri, then sat back on his wobbly chair. "Carole worked for Macpherson."

"Doing what?" I asked.

Before I could get a reply, the waitress, a vision whose tawny hair resembled a muskrat recently flattened by a steamroller, returned with Yates's liquid confection. Hand noticeably trembling, he took a longish snort of the vile-looking concoction, cast some more furtive glances around the café, then inhaled magnificently, as if psyching himself up for an Olympic pole vault. "After they met at Nirvana... well, you know Carole. She had a hard time holding down a job. She was pretty unhappy working in the centre, something about the owner trying to control her mind through astral projection. Anyway, I think Macpherson had a thing for her—"

"You know, Donald," I said, interrupting, "I find it hard to believe Macpherson would have anything to do with a place like Nirvana. He doesn't strike me as the New Age type."

"I don't know. I never met him. Carole said he was probably on the look-out for young girls. Places like Nirvana attract them in droves."

"She said that and she still went to work for him?"

"Like I said, she'd just about had it at Nirvana. And, besides, Macpherson offered her some pretty good money."

"I'll ask again," I said. "Doing what?"

"Macpherson brought back all these books and manuscripts from England and needed someone to help him sort through them. I guess he needed a secretary or something."

I frowned. "That kind of job is usually reserved for graduate students, isn't it? As far as I know, Carole had a bachelor of science from Queen's. Hardly the qualifications for English scholarship."

"I wouldn't know," Yates said. "All I do know is that she started working for him in June."

"The last time you saw her," I broke in.

"Well, not exactly. I did see her after that. There was somebody else... and a tape..." Just then Yates gulped audibly, his eyes riveted to the passing scene outside. "Excuse me... alcohol goes right through me." He got up abruptly and headed for the back, where I gathered the men's room was.

"Maybe one of us should go with him," Jerry suggested.

"Now who's lost in a forties detective film?" I said as I peered out the café window. Nothing unusual, as far as I could see. "Maybe you're right, though. C'mon." I plunked some money on the table and got to my feet.

"You're determined to make me sweat, aren't you?" Jerry grumbled petulantly, popping a chocolate mint into his mouth.

"You're the one who's interested in *Cardenio*. Yates is a hot lead, and you know it."

Reluctantly Jerry hoisted himself to his feet and lumbered after me, but not quickly enough. The washroom was empty. Jerry and I headed for the back door, pulled it open, and plunged into an alley. There was only one way out— toward Queen Street. When we reached the sidewalk, I caught a glimpse of Yates dashing around an eastbound Queen car.

"C'mon, Jerry, there he goes!" I shouted, turning around. Jerry was leaning against a brick wall, a beached whale.

"I think I'll just rest here, if you don't mind. I'm like Oscar Wilde. 'I nauseate walking: 'tis a country diversion. I loathe the country.'"

"Sounds more like what a character says in Congreve's *Way of the World*, Jerry."

He winced between puffs. "Smart asses nauseate me, too, Mickey. You'd better get going if you want to catch our friend."

Without another word I whirled and sprinted after the streetcar, which was now lurching down the track. Fortunately traffic was pretty heavy and it wasn't making much headway. I figured I'd catch up to it at the next stop. Out of shape as I was, I just made it to the corner as the streetcar jerked to a halt. Climbing on, I paid the driver and threaded my way through the packed car, intent on spotting Yates.

The streetcar was one of the articulated jobs and quite long. When I reached the accordion-like ligature, I still hadn't found my quarry. And no wonder. With Toronto's multi-ethnic citizenry crammed elbow to elbow, I could barely see my feet, let alone Mr. Bunny. Then I spied him! He was near the rear exit, and his pasty face was sheathed in sweat. His eyes popped and, as he edged closer to the exit, he stared in what could only be called horror at something or someone I couldn't see. Then Yates saw me. By this time I was a few feet from him. He was mouthing something. I strained to hear it, wishing I could read lips. It sounded like Vim or Vic.

"The tape," he finally gasped. "Get the tape."

"What tape?" I cried over the people blocking my way.

"He's here," Yates whispered, glancing behind him again. "Vip."

And that was that. The streetcar had come to a stop, and I knew Yates was going to bolt. As I struggled to reach him, a swarthy, wiry little man with the face of a malevolent cartoon character slammed against Yates, knocking him off balance. The blond sales clerk tumbled out of the door along with his assailant.

Actually they weren't the only ones to cartwheel out of the streetcar. As I clawed my way after Yates and his gym buddy, I took a sizable number of the citizenry with me, and not all of them wanted to get off. By the time I untangled myself from a heap of cursing bodies, Yates was hotfooting northward up Spadina Avenue, the cartoon midget in close pursuit. Then they vanished into one of the largest crowds I'd ever seen on the wide avenue that still served as the main artery of the city's garment district.

This was Chinatown, too, and it looked as if some kind of parade, fair, or demonstration was in progress. Thousands of people milled around dozens of tables and booths. As I ploughed through the excited throng, I searched frantically for Yates's blond head. If the crowd was bad here, it would only get worse as I got closer to Dundas Street, the nerve centre of Chinatown. It was tough going, a little like swimming upstream, but eventually I reached an island of relative calm in front of a kung-fu movie house emblazoned with an enormous two-storey bas-relief of a golden dragon. All kinds of kites— butterflies, birds, dragons, even centipedes— festooned many of the booths and tables. Other booths sold food, mostly Chinese snacks like shrimp and beef dumplings, duck webs, spring rolls, and crêpes stuffed with pork and stir-fried vegetables.

But I didn't have time to enjoy the festivities. Scanning the mob, I thought I glimpsed a blond head above the hundreds of people in front of me. Like a barracuda, I sliced through the crowd, making my way to the expansive sidewalk across the street. Just as I put my foot on the curb, I heard a chorus of screams and was pushed aside by a panicked populace.

I ended up in the gutter along with several other people and a table full of overripe papayas, guavas, melons, and numerous unidentifiable exotic fruits. All I managed to see was the flash of a car barrelling down the sidewalk. All I heard were cries and shouts and the crunch of something more than just wood and metal.

As soon as I got back on my feet, I bulled through the crowd toward the source of the worst moans and cries. Several people lay on the pavement, a few with broken limbs, others with cuts and gashes. One was perfectly still. He lay on his stomach amid what had probably been a rack of skinned ducks. There was blood and gore everywhere. Some of it undoubtedly came from Donald Yates.

Looking up, I spotted the cartoon character. In an instant, though, he was lost in the crowd, his pipe-cleaner legs carrying him as fast as they could northward to wherever the long-vanished murder car awaited him. There was no point in running after him, so I stooped to one knee, hoping Yates might still be able to talk. But no dice. I was no expert in death, but I was pretty sure the blond sales clerk was never going to say anything ever again.

I straightened and moved away from the carnage. All hell had broken out on Spadina. The crowd was already making way for a couple of ambulances arriving on the scene. Uniformed police, who had obviously been keeping an eye on the festivities before the killer car began its rampage, worked hard to keep the mob away from the injured and maimed.

"Are... you... all right?" a voice asked with some difficulty at my shoulder. It was Jerry.

I turned and looked at him. His broad brow was sweaty and his big chin shuddered with each breath.

"I was—"

For a moment I thought Jerry was actually going to express more concern for my well-being, but he quickly regained his usual composure.

"Don't tell me you were worried about me," I quipped.

Jerry unfurled an eyebrow and squinted at me. "You do need a keeper, Mickey, but I'm not applying for the job."

"Then why are you all out of breath? You should see yourself."

"Just my old asthma kicking up."

"Sure," I said, grinning.

Jerry glared at me. "You're a mess. You look like a fruit salad."

I glanced at the late Donald Yates, who was now being trundled into an ambulance. "Better that than Welsh rarebit. What's going on here, Jerry? A fair of some kind?"

"Chung Yang," he replied. Jerry lived and breathed Chinatown. I knew he'd know the score. "It's one of the Chinese festivals of the dead. You see all these kites? The idea is to buy one and fly it from the highest possible place. Apparently the festival was inspired by some Chinese Cassandra way back when who warned of an impending disaster. You're supposed to head for the hills and fly a kite."

Jerry and I watched as the ambulance carrying Yates's broken body moved off. "What's it all about, Mickey?"

"Murder," I muttered. "Pure and simple."

"Level with me. Has this got something to do with *Cardenio*?"

"I don't know. But there's a tape somewhere. Before he got slam-dunked under the car Yates told me to get it."

"A tape? You mean a videotape?"

"I wish I knew." I looked toward the lake. The shaft of the CN Tower stood sentinel as always. Maybe I should buy a kite, I thought, and beat it to the top before things got worse.

As I slid a smear of papaya from my hair, I saw a couple of grim-looking cops moving toward us. "Get out your dance card, Jerry. Here come the local gendarmes."

STATION X

"What do you mean you don't know? You're supposed to be a fucking hotshot reporter, aren't you?"

The speaker was Detective Sergeant Eddie Fournier, a smartly dressed plainclothes cop who looked more like a Bay Street banker or broker than a policeman. I was getting to be quite the habitué of cop shops and thought I'd write a tour guide one of these days, especially now that I'd hit the jackpot— the dreaded 52 Division on Dundas West.

"I told you," I mumbled for the umpteenth time. "It happened too fast and I was more concerned about my own skin. I think it was a Mercedes or a BMW, but I'm not sure."

"Hey, you drive a BMW, Eddie," one of the other cops in the windowless interrogation room cracked.

Fournier seared the guy with an acetylene-torch look, then glared at me. "A Mercedes or a BMW? My, my, hit men are getting more upscale every day. Shit, Finnegan, can't you tell the difference?"

"Remind me to renew my subscription to *Car and Driver* as soon as I get a driver's licence."

Either Fournier was getting real steamed or the extra-high collar on his pale yellow pinstriped silk shirt was too tight; a vein on the side of his tanned neck popped as if it had been goosed by a cattle prod. "You know, I hated you when you were digging up dirt for the *Globe* and I hate you even more now that you seem mixed up with every fucking murder that goes down in this city. For two cents I'd—"

"Take me out to Cherry Beach and play soccer with me?" I horned in. "That wouldn't go with the GQ image, Fournier. You might even mess up that nice blue suit of yours. Hugo Boss, isn't it?"

The wiseacre who'd piped up about Fournier's BMW smirked. "Eddie always wears blue and grey. Just like in a bank. Says any other colour's for proles."

Fournier straightened his burgundy silk tie, shoved a well-manicured hand through his blond, blow-dried locks, and smiled icily. "Gorman, if you want to break into comedy, waste Yuk-Yuk's time, not mine." The staff sergeant might have looked like a million bucks, but he talked a plugged nickel.

"I think he's pretty funny, Eddie," I said.

Fournier drilled me with his Black and Decker eyes. "Finnegan, just tell me why the Yates stiff has to be murder. People get run over accidentally all the time. Hell, a whole lot of people got bowled over besides Yates today."

"Sure, people are run over on the sidewalk in the middle of a fair every day. I mean, what's so amazing about a guy being pushed out of a streetcar by a character who looks as if he were drawn by a spacey Walt Disney with a snootful of coke?"

"Read the papers, Finnegan. All kinds of fucking crazy things happen in this shithole of a city. People walk down the street and a fridge flattens them from some highrise. Somebody else ignites spontaneously in bed and turns into a pile of cinders. Face it, hack. Accidents happen."

Now that hurt. Just when I thought Eddie and I were really getting to like each other, he had cast doubt on my professional integrity. "Yeah, I know, Fournier. Like some guys go into a restaurant and blow away a few patrons for fun. Or a bunch of teens ventilate the populace from their car window. Or better still, something you'd appreciate, Eddie. Some cops get caught pimping and drug-pushing on the side and end up offing one of their junkies when she gets too strung out and threatens to rat on them."

If Eddie had had a baseball bat just then, my head would have been ricocheting off a building in downtown Buffalo in no time flat.

"You said his name was Vip, didn't you?" Frank Kaplan asked, no doubt saving a few of my vital organs. When I'd been hauled into the station with Jerry, I'd dropped my fairy copfather's name, hoping it would get me out of 52 Division before daybreak. Jerry had dropped the name of a Forest Hill lawyer friend and was ushered out the door instantly.

"Kaplan," Fournier growled, "you're Robbery, I'm Homicide. That means I ask the questions, you observe. Got it?"

"Yeah, I got it."

"Okay, Finnegan," Fournier said, sighing, "you've got a point with this guy Vip. We've got him ID'ed as Lupo Vip, a flipped-out hood from Montreal. The guy originally got his jollies in Romania. Transylvania, if you can believe it. Even had a few working vacations in Bosnia. We don't have a photo of him, but who needs it? He looks like a cross between the Alka-Seltzer kid and the Pillsbury dough boy."

"I kind of thought he took after Gumby myself."

"Vip's bad news. Even worse, he's connected to a friend of yours, Nik Rorke."

I'd been drinking Alberta tar sands coffee when Fournier laid that name on me. I nearly got it all over his nice blue suit.

"Maybe we should pay Mr. Shaw another visit," Kaplan suggested.

Fournier scowled. "There you go again, Kaplan. Didn't I—"

"Sergeant, I'm investigating the theft of that Shakespeare manuscript. Yates worked for Shaw. Rorke's been seen with Shaw. Vip is tight with Rorke. When I add all that up, Sergeant, that makes Yates's *murder* my business."

Fournier rolled his eyes and stared at the ceiling. "Gorman, make some more coffee. This is going to be a long night."

I winked at Kaplan. "Before you start playing volleyball with my brains again, Fournier, tell me one thing. Where do you buy your sun lamps?"

It took me a while, but I finally got out of there in one piece. Kaplan escorted me to the street and waited on the wide sidewalk until a cab arrived. We stood in the cold Chinatown air and looked up at the orangish sky.

"Never can see any stars in this goddamn city," Kaplan muttered.

"Yeah," I grunted, pulling my jacket collar up. "Maybe we should move to the country. People don't get killed there as much."

"Don't count on it," Kaplan said, tightening the belt on his brown topcoat. "You know, Mickey, Hammer Harry's still out there."

"What?"

"Herbert Sutcliffe's hammer doesn't match up with the one Harry uses. And it doesn't match up with the one used on Sharon Praeger."

I stared hard at Kaplan's cratered face. "Wait a minute. That goes without saying if it doesn't match up with Harry's other killings, unless..."

"Yeah, you got it. We're pretty sure Harry didn't do the Praeger woman, either."

"Maybe he bought a new hammer."

"Sure. But Harry's a methodical monster who likes to tenderize his victims just so. Then there's the semen."

"It's different?"

"No, there was none. Harry always leaves semen— plenty of it. A lot of rapists these days use condoms, what with semen analysis and DNA profiles, but not Harry. It's his calling card, like he's proud of how much he can generate. He leaves it all over his victims. Whoever raped and killed Praeger used a condom. It took Forensic a while, but they're pretty sure we've got a copycat. Which is all we need in this city at the moment."

"I suppose you checked Herbie's semen."

"You bet. No dice. He may be somebody's fiend, but he's not ours."

My cab pulled up and I got in.

"Mickey," Kaplan called out before the driver shifted into gear.

"Yeah?" I said, leaning out the open window.

"You watch out, okay?"

"I'm just looking for a girl, Sergeant."

"Yeah, I know. That's what bothers me. Like I said, you can't see the goddamn stars at night in this town."

The cab rolled off down the street. I twisted around and looked out the back window. Kaplan stood on the sidewalk, dwarfed by the concrete bunker cop shop, his shoulders hunched, his face obscured by his battered brown fedora. Maybe he was squinting up at the sky. But who could tell in the blaze of neon Chinese that lit up Dundas Street?

I slept a good chunk of the next day and then remembered that I'd been invited to dinner at Jack and Brigit's. After buying a bottle of DeLoach white zinfandel at the liquor store, figuring it would be a safe bet since I didn't know what we'd be eating, I trudged over to Jack's house, fully intent on having a little R and R.

While I waited on Jack's porch for someone to answer my knock, I thought about Sharon Praeger and Donald Yates, Carole's dead friends. The odds against Carole herself still being alive were getting higher and higher. Who was behind the murders? More to the point, though, was why? But before I could ponder that riddle, the door opened.

Brigit stood in the doorway in her usual glory. Tonight she wore white chinos and an oversized white Russian peasant blouse. For some reason I thought of Anna Karenina, though why I don't know. Anna Karenina, whether played by Greta Garbo or not, would hardly have worn a peasant blouse. And, besides, Brigit was no troubled lover about to throw herself under a train. She had everything a woman could possibly want. She was everything a man dreamed about. Maybe I was just feeling guilty about not finishing Tolstoy's novel.

"You're always so pensive on our porch," she said to me, a curious smile tickling her lipstickless lips.

I grinned. "That's because I do my best thinking here. It's inspirational."

"Come in, Mickey. Supper's just about ready."

I followed her down the hallway and into the kitchen at the back of the house. Jack was tending a wok on the stove. He was wearing the loudest pair of Bermuda shorts I'd ever seen, sort of what Jackson Pollock might have designed had he been Yves St. Laurent's protégé instead of a painter. A Hawaiian shirt featuring Mauna Loa in all its splendour only made matters worse. Polyester Stockhausen.

"Blinded by the light," I said. "Where did you pick up that ensemble, Jack? A Zellers in Hell?"

Jack looked up from his culinary ministrations. "We're having Polynesian tonight and I believe in dressing for the food. Is that wine you've got there, Mickey?"

"You bet." I handed the plastic bag to him.

He pulled out the bottle and examined the label. "Yuppie rosé! Really, Mickey, you amaze me. I thought he-man hootch like tequila and beer was more your style."

"If you two are finished trashing each other's taste," Brigit said, "maybe one of you big, strong men can set the table and the other can open that bottle of wine. I'm dying for a drink."

"Allow me," I said, winking at Jack.

"Are you sure you want to trust Mickey with such a delicate operation, Brigit? Remember when I had that party to commemorate my being passed over a third time for a full professorship? He opened that expensive French champagne and unleashed Krakatoa. And then there was the time he took an hour to dig out the cork in a bottle of d'Yquem. I remember Laura—"

Brigit glared at her husband as she handed me a corkscrew. Pasting a silly, insincere grin on my face, I twirled the corkscrew like a six-gun, tore off the foil at the top of the bottle in one strip, jabbed the corkscrew into the cork, and produced the requisite *thwock!*

"Bravo!" Brigit cried, and both she and Jack gave me a round of applause.

Then Jack stopped clapping and said, "I should have gotten out my camcorder. We may never again see such a feat in our lifetimes."

"You have a camcorder?" I asked incredulously. "I didn't think you were the videophile type."

Brigit snorted. "Are you kidding, Mickey? Jack loves toys. Thank God, though, he's gotten beyond the March of Time stage. When he first got the camcorder, not long after Conor was born, I was living with a mechanical voyeur."

"Jack, the home video freak. Who would have believed it?" I said as I poured out three glasses of wine. "I hope you guys have more vino. I don't imagine this will last us long."

"Does Hawaii have tourists?" Jack asked, anointing his concoction with soy sauce.

"What's with all this sudden interest in Hawaii, Jack?" I asked.

"I'm thinking of retiring there. You know, buy myself a ranch. Indulge my vices."

"That's my husband," Brigit trilled. "Gentleman gaucho."

"Gauchos are in Argentina, ma chère, or since we're guzzling California, babe."

"Always the professor," Brigit mumbled as she sliced up mangoes, avocadoes, various nuts, Boston lettuce, cherry tomatoes, and mandarin oranges and tossed them into a large glass bowl.

"Chow time," Jack announced, spooning some of his creation into his mouth.

It was quite the feast. Besides the salad we had homemade pita, basmati rice, and Jack's gourmet poi-poi. We polished off the zinfandel and broke open a bottle of white Burgundy.

"I'd like to make a toast," I said, raising my glass just before Brigit got up to serve dessert, which was bananas flambéed in rum. "To my two favourite people— Jack and Brigit Malone."

"Flattery will get you everywhere," Brigit said, beaming.

"Really?" I said, lost in thought for a moment. I was a little amazed at what my mind was contemplating. "Will it get me a coffee?" I asked quickly.

"Your wish is our command," Brigit said, jumping to her feet. "Will a cappuccino do?"

My eyes widened. "Does Bill Clinton crave co-eds?"

Jack had gone into the living room to stack a few more CDs into the stereo. When he came back, I said, "Has to be Roland Kirk." The unmistakable squawk of many saxes sailed into the dining room.

"You know me, Mickey. A connoisseur of eccentrics, especially in jazz. Speaking of the less than normal, how's your Holy Grail going? Any news on the damsel in distress?"

I frowned. "It's not funny, Jack. Bodies are piling up. All of them Carole's friends."

The Yates killing had made the papers and television.

"Did you find out anything from Yates?" Jack asked.

"Yeah, a few things. Carole worked for Macpherson on the *Cardenio* package."

"Wow!" Jack whistled. "You've got your connection."

"Sure, but damned if I know where it all leads."

"You think she's dead, don't you?" Brigit asked from the kitchen, her beautiful green eyes filled with concern.

I looked at her but didn't answer. "Mmm, I smell coffee."

"Three cappuccinos and flambéed bananas coming right up," Brigit said, trying to inject some cheer into her throaty voice.

"So you don't think Hammer Harry did in Sharon Praeger?" Jack asked. He had fished out a bottle of Metaxa seven-star brandy and was pouring it into three snifters.

"Neither do the cops. Kaplan told me the hammers don't match. And the DNA and semen tests don't jibe, either. Apparently Harry likes to smear his victims with his semen. And there were no traces of semen found in or on Sharon. As for Herbie Sutcliffe, that maniac they scooped up with me in High Park, he seems to be in the clear."

"He still could have killed Sharon Praeger, no?"

"Maybe. But the cops are pretty doubtful. The hammer he was carrying doesn't match the one used on Sharon. Still, they should lock up the guy and throw away the key. With Herbie it's tick, tick, tick and only a matter of time."

Jack swirled his brandy. "Ah... what else did Yates tell you?"

"What makes you think he told me anything?"

"I know you, Mickey. There's more."

"He said something about a tape."

"Really?" Jack said, drinking a little brandy.

Brigit dished out dessert and served the coffee.

"What's on the tape and what connection it has to anything else is a blank to me," I said.

"It's all about *Cardenio,* isn't it?"

"Sure as hell seems like it."

"Have you talked to Macpherson about Carole?"

"I wish. I've left messages all over the place for him. He seems to have gone fishing."

Just then the phone rang. Shoving a spoonful of already-cooling flambéed banana into his mouth, Jack pushed away from the oak farmhouse table and trotted out to the living room.

"One of Jack's admirers, no doubt," I said, grinning at Brigit.

Her eyes widened tremendously, as if I'd told her baby Conor had been run over by a truck. Raw panic paraded across her usually buoyant face. But it was over in a split second.

"Are you okay, Brigit?"

"Uh... sure. The bananas are still too hot. I think I burned my tongue."

I didn't buy it. Something was bothering her. The little scar near the corner of her mouth twitched slightly. "Is everything all right with you and Jack?"

"W-why do you ask?"

"Reporter's instinct. It's like riding a bike. It never leaves you. Besides, you and Jack did have some rough times a few years back, didn't you?"

"Yes... but, Mickey, that was a long time ago. Jack and I are fine."

"Yeah, sure you are. Don't mind me. This *Cardenio* business and Carole Rutland have got me looking for gremlins everywhere."

"You think Jack's a gremlin?"

I laughed. "He can be a little overbearing sometimes, but Jack's no monster. He's too..."

"Lovable?"

"Yeah, lovable." I finished off my bananas, took a sip of cappuccino, and studied Brigit's face. It was composed, almost serious. "You know, I've always wondered about that little scar of yours, the one near your mouth. How did you get it?"

Brigit raised one long, tapered hand to her lips. "This?" Thunderclouds hove into her eyes again. I was getting good at causing this goddess grief. "You know my mother was... was institutionalized."

"Yeah. You told me years ago. That's how Jack got the inspiration for his book of poems, *White on White*."

"And how I got interested in psychology. We used to visit her as much as we could."

"Why was she in the hospital?"

"She..." A sob threatened to drown Brigit's words. "She killed my father with a butcher knife."

I sat back on the colonial chair, which creaked ominously. "I... you never told me that before. I'm sorry."

Brigit smiled sadly. "Why are you sorry, Mickey? It was a long, long time ago. She's dead. As for the scar, well, I've had it since I was eight or nine, before my mother... She hit me with an iron. She didn't like the way I ironed one of her blouses. Can you imagine?"

I chugalugged some brandy and coughed. "What about your father? What was he like?" I bit my tongue. I couldn't stop myself. Mickey de Torquemada. Bring out the thumbscrews.

Brigit's right hand twisted the gold chain of the jade necklace she was wearing. "My father?" she whispered. But that was it. Her lovely green gaze flew around the room like an exotic bird seeking escape. She had the necklace in knots.

At that moment Jack returned to the kitchen. "So who's the mystery caller?" I asked, overjoyed at his arrival. It saved Brigit from the rack.

If a wisecrack had a face, it would have looked like Jack. But not then. His features now looked as if they'd been given the works by a Calvinist mortician. Mausoleums stared at us from the doorway, not merriment.

"What's wrong, Jack?" Brigit asked, alarm in her voice.

Jack sat down heavily and took a long swig of brandy. I'd never seen him so shaken up. "That was Avery Brownlee on the phone. I can't believe it."

"Can't believe what?" I prompted impatiently.

"Macpherson. Garrett Macpherson's dead. They found him at the foot of Robarts Library. He must have jumped off."

STATION XI

Fort Book. That's what some U of T students call Robarts Library. Approaching the corner of Harbord and Huron streets and looking up at the behemoth's beige concrete brutalism, I had to agree with the nickname. The building bristled with Modernist ramparts and towers, causing one to wonder at the mentality that deemed it necessary to encase knowledge in a monolith. Perhaps the architects had taken *2001: A Space Odyssey* too literally. Still, as Jack and I made our way through the drizzle toward Robarts, I had to admit this bastard child of Le Corbusier did have a certain presence. With thunder grumbling in the distance, occasional flashes of lightning, and its towers wreathed in mist, Robarts was the perfect place to witness dark deeds.

When Avery Brownlee called, Garrett Macpherson's body had just been found, and the police were still swarming over the grass surrounding the library as Jack and I arrived. Jack had insisted on coming with me, which I found mystifying. Macpherson was hardly one of his favourite people. But maybe there's a bit of ghoul in all of us.

There was quite a crowd gathered around the little stylized raw concrete gazebo off to one side of Robarts. At least I assumed the structure was meant to suggest a gazebo. Who could tell what the megalithic myrmidons of Robarts really had in mind? For one crazy moment as I wiped rain out of my eyes, I thought the figures encircling the gazebo, most of whom were garbed in yellow slickers, were some kind of New Age cult bent on celebrating concrete. Wine always did go to my head.

"Hey, hey, the gang's all here," Eddie Fournier said as Jack and I reached the gazebo. He was standing next to Frank Kaplan, who nodded at me, and half a dozen other cops, both plainclothes and uniforms.

"You must really crack them up at funerals, Eddie," I snapped, noting the detective sergeant's black leather raincoat with envy.

"Tell me, Finnegan," Fournier growled, "how is it that you always manage to turn up when someone dies? And who's the bird with you this time? Not your pal, the walking side of beef, that's for sure."

"Uh, Sergeant," a voice creaked behind Fournier, "the gentleman with

Mr. Finnegan is Jack Malone, a member of our department. I telephoned some of poor Garrett's colleagues." Avery Brownlee's few strands of white hair were stuck to his skull as if glued, and his translucent lips wriggled like mating grubs as he tried to fix his incessantly twitching eyes on Fournier. He looked elderly and panic-stricken, a man who had been left out in the rain too long.

"That explains your new sidekick, Finnegan," Fournier finally said. "What about you?"

"I was a dinner guest, Sergeant."

Fournier pulled a pack of Player's out of his raincoat, extracted a cigarette, and stuck it in his mouth. "Natch. Anybody got a light? I forgot my lighter." One of the uniforms tossed a Bic disposable to Fournier and he lit his cigarette.

While Fournier and I were playing verbal footsie, Brownlee steered Jack away from the throng around the gazebo. Brownlee seemed overjoyed to speak with someone other than a cop. Meanwhile Fournier sucked on his cigarette and went into a huddle with the other cops, allowing me to crane my head skyward to look at the top of Robarts, fourteen storeys above me. There wasn't much point, though. Despite the lights, the upper floors of Fort Book were obscured by the steady drizzle.

"What's Fournier's problem?" I asked Kaplan as he drew alongside.

"Eddie's bucking for inspector. Gives him a permanent burr up his ass." Kaplan looked up at the library. "Not a pretty way to go, eh?"

"Must have been quite a mess when he landed."

"You're lucky. The meat wagon's already been here. He hit that concrete thing over there—" he pointed at the gazebo "— and bounced off. Lots of eyewitnesses. The library's still open. Actually, he couldn't have dived off the main building. If he had, he would have whacked those trees instead of the concrete gizmo. We figure he took the header off that."

I glanced at the six-storey mini-tower Kaplan was pointing at. "The Fisher Rare Book Library."

"Yeah."

Then I looked at the gazebo and saw the outline of a man in white tape on the grass nearby.

"That's where he ended up. Most of him, anyway."

I glared at Kaplan. "Too bad you can't show me an eight-by-ten colour glossy."

"It can be arranged. A lot of people are dead, Mickey."

"Yeah, tell me about it. So what's the deal with Macpherson?"

"Suicide, obviously."

"Sure, and Yates was an accident and one of TO's many maniacs offed Sharon Praeger."

"We found a suicide note in Macpherson's pocket. The lab will have to go over it, but we showed it to Brownlee and he says it's Macpherson's handwriting, all right."

"So he took a dive off the library. But why? Because he couldn't live without his precious *Cardenio*? Give me a break."

Kaplan doffed his brown fedora and shook the rain off it, a useless gesture, it seemed to me. When he put it back on, it still looked like a drowned rat. "Let's just say the note's interesting."

"Can I see it?"

"Lab boys have it. But I scribbled down what it said." He pulled out a dog-eared black notepad. "Let's get under that ledge over there so I can get out of the rain."

We moved over to the ledge where there was a floodlight, and Kaplan handed me the notepad. I stared at the words he'd scrawled:

> I shall fall
> Like a bright exhalation in the evening,
> And no man see me more.
> For falseness must reap its grim harvest
> And evil its just deserts.

When I finished reading the blank verse, I looked up at Kaplan quizzically.

"Brownlee says it's Shakespeare. He even went into the library to check it. The first few lines are from *Henry VIII*. The last bit, though, is a mystery. It sounds like Shakespeare, Brownlee says, but as far as he can tell, it's not in anything the guy wrote. He even double-checked in a computer con— what the hell did he call it?"

"Concordance?"

"Yeah, that's it."

I broke out in a grin. I couldn't help it. There was something funny about a big, battered palooka with a broken nose holding forth on Shakespeare in the rain at the scene of a supposed suicide.

"What's so funny?" he asked.

"I should have gotten you to *read* the note to me. I bet you're a regular Olivier when it comes to blank verse."

"Let me tell you, Mickey. This is as close to Shakespeare as I ever want to get. He's bad for the health."

I stared at Kaplan's big face. I'd seen prettier mugs on a moose, but the guy had brains. For all I knew, he recited English metaphysical poetry in the shower. "So what's the score? You think Macpherson stole his own manuscript? If he did, where is it? I can't see a guy like that arranging to have people knocked off. Somehow the idea of Nik Rorke and Macpherson as teammates doesn't jibe."

"Who said anything about Macpherson stealing anything? Maybe he faked the whole thing. Maybe this whole business is a lot of hot air. Maybe he just couldn't live with what he'd done, knew he couldn't get away with the scam much longer."

"I don't buy it. Way back before Sharon and Yates got bumped off I thought Macpherson might have faked *Cardenio*. It all sounded too good to be true. But this many people don't get killed because of forgery. There's got to be more to it."

"Maybe Praeger and Yates were going to blow the whistle."

"What are you telling me? The cops now think it's all wrapped up neatly? Case closed?"

"He had black marks all over his hands. Macpherson, I mean."

"So?"

"So maybe it means something. We'll know more in the morning. My guess, it's ink. Same as the kind in the suicide note."

"Great. Macpherson was a sloppy writer. I still don't think he took a dive off the Fisher by himself."

"Do you see murder everywhere, Mickey?"

"Only when it's there."

"Listen, about Carole Rutland."

"Yeah?"

"I couldn't dig up anything. A total blank. It doesn't look good."

"What about family? She's got a mother somewhere."

"Can't find her, either. It's damn frustrating."

The ring of cops around the gazebo— which, on closer inspection, turned out to be a Pollution Probe time capsule— was starting to break up, with the constables heading back to their patrol cars. Even the crowd of rubbernecking students and passersby had grown bored of ogling the huddle of cops. Jack left Brownlee's side and came over to where Kaplan and I were standing. "I'm heading home, Mickey."

"What did Brownlee want?" I asked.

"He and Macpherson were pretty close. He's really shaken up. And now the cops are going to drag him into the station for more questions. The old guy needed a friendly face to talk to, even if I am the black sheep of the department."

I looked at Kaplan. "If it's a cut-and-dried suicide, what do you guys want with Brownlee?"

"I'm Robbery, remember, not Homicide. But my guess would be it has something to do with Brownlee being on the premises when Macpherson jumped."

"Brownlee was on the rooftop?" I asked, surprised.

"Whoa, Mickey, I didn't say that. He was *in* the old book joint."

"Well," Jack said, digging something out of his ear, "I guess English scholarship has lost one of its true giants."

"The guy's dead, Jack," I said.

"Yes, isn't he? I knew the patronizing bastard was a phony."

"Brownlee told you about the note?"

"Sure, one last academic flourish. Leave it to Macpherson to pick a library to sail off after dispensing a little *authentic* Shakespeare."

"Half Shakespeare," I corrected.

"Yeah, half. Still, you'd think the clown would have used a speech by Buckingham instead of Cardinal Wolsey. The cardinal died of natural causes, but Buckingham got the chop."

"You think Macpherson was executed?"

"Executed? You mean, as in Mafia? Hell, no! It just seems to me that if you're going to be ass enough to take a swan dive set to Shakespeare, you might as well identify with a violent death. Then again, I always thought Macpherson was a shitty scholar with a Lucifer complex. I gotta go, Mickey. Brigit's waiting up."

As I watched Jack shuffle off into the drizzle, something kept nagging at me. *And no two such as these, the clown and the buffoon, shall we see when comes the reckoning.* Where had I heard that? It was something else that had sounded Shakespearean yet wasn't. Or was it?

"We're all finished here, Sergeant, top and bottom," Fournier said to Kaplan, interrupting my reverie. "You coming back to the division with me?"

"Mickey thinks it's murder, Eddie."

"I don't want to hear it, Kaplan. I got a nice little suicide. The note's too damn vague and artsy-fartsy for my taste, but these college types would rather scramble their brains on the pavement than talk straight. And you, Kaplan, you've got this Shakespeare biz sewn up. So don't tell me what this two-bit skid-row news vulture thinks. I couldn't care less."

"Hey, Eddie," I said, "you better get out of this rain. It's hell on leather."

Fournier glanced at his rain-speckled coat. "Fuck! C'mon, Kaplan, let's go. We've got a shitload of paperwork to wade through." The detective sergeant turned to me. "As for you, Finnegan, go peddle some tabloids."

Kaplan shrugged and headed into the gloom with the dapper, drenched Fournier. They made a nice pair. Sort of like Godzilla and Bambi, only I didn't know which was which. What did Duncan say in *Macbeth* about men? "There's no art to find the mind's construction in the face." Yeah, sure, and look what happened to him. I was getting more depressed by the minute. The murk was getting murkier. But the cops were happy at least.

I looked southward toward the lake. I couldn't see the CN Tower, but it was there, its warning lights winking madly in the night. Appearances weren't just deceiving; they were downright debilitating. My brain was mush. It was time to hit the hay and dream a few things that weren't dreamt in my philosophy, or in hell. But before I departed, I sauntered over to the Pollution Probe gazebo to read the plaque I'd noticed earlier. "In the hope," it said, "that this time capsule will be found by a civilization wiser than our own, we have buried here a record of man's folly." Well, I thought, Macpherson sure knew how to pick his spots. Or someone did.

When I got home, the red light on my message machine was blinking. I got a lot of mileage out of the old gadget, a leftover from my upwardly mobile days. Probably the first time in half a year I'd actually come home to find someone had called. Mind you, I was always forgetting to turn the damn thing on. As I punched the play button, I made a mental note to haul the bloody gizmo down to the nearest pawnshop. I could use a few bucks.

The machine whirred and clicked and then spat out its oracle. "Mickey, it's Jerry. Can't you come up with something a little more original for your message?" Good old Jer, I thought. Always the critic. "Listen, it's about 8:30. Someone called at the paper and left a message for me. I'm supposed to go out to the Junction at midnight. A real hot tip about *Cardenio,* the message says. There's an abandoned meat-packer out there on Ethel Avenue. I knew an Ethel once. Pretty high-proof, she was. Place has a billboard with an animal orchestra on it. I kid you not. Gentleman says the thieves are using it for their warehouse. I thought you might like to tag along with me. I'll meet you at Runnymede and Ryding, just south of St. Clair. Can't miss the corner— there's a giant pine rocking chair on top of a furniture store. Say quarter to twelve? *Hasta luego.*"

I groaned and looked at my watch. It was 11:35. The last thing in the world I wanted to do was to trek out into the night again. Bed and bourbon beckoned, but I didn't relish the idea of Jerry looking over the warehouse by himself.

Cursing, I called a cab, then raided the cupboard for the mickey of bourbon I'd stashed for emergencies. This late-night assignation sure as hell qualified. Rooting through my never-used camping gear, I found a plastic flask and dumped the bourbon into it. Thus fortified, I waited for the taxi.

When I climbed into the cab a few minutes later and told the driver my destination, he looked at me thoughtfully. "The stockyards is all closed up now, ain't they? You workin' a night shift at Canada Packers or somethin'?"

"Yeah, you could say that," I mumbled as we splashed through the nearly deserted streets.

"Pays pretty good, I hear. Dirty, though, I guess."

A chatty cab driver, I thought. That's all I need. "Blood and blood and more blood," I intoned.

"Huh?"

"The Caruso of the carving knife, they call me. Sweeney Todd, look out."

The cabbie took his eye off the road and stared at me, a worried furrow creasing his substantial forehead. The rest of the ride transpired in peace.

We hit the corner of Keele and Dundas West—the heart of the Junction. The city's massive stockyards had been located north of here, as well as most of its meat-packing. In the Junction, all rail lines and roads converged in a tangle of transportation. The crossroads to end all crossroads. Once upon a time it had been hell on wheels, this part of town, what with railway workers, stockmen, meat-packers, and all. Little Chicago in Toronto the Good. Almost singlehandedly responsible for the temperance tantrums in the early part of the century, the dry revolution that once rolled over all of Ontario.

Now, as I glanced out the cab window, the old neighbourhood looked pretty depressed and dilapidated. A lot of the old industrial areas of the city were like that. Some of the trains still rolled, but cows and pigs and other four-footed beasts didn't give up their guts for the supper table any more. A much smaller stockyard had been built somewhere else for the few meat eaters left.

Long ago, when I first started out on my climb to newsprint Olympia, I'd done an exposé on the meat-packing business, some of whose players were doing funny things with meat. So I was all too familiar with the Junction and its olfactory delights.

Finally the cab pulled up at the corner of Runnymede and Ryding. Sure enough, there was a king-sized rocking chair perched on the roof of a low-slung building. I paid the cab driver, got out, and watched with some trepidation as the taxi accelerated away into the dank dark. From the expression on the driver's face, I was pretty sure he was more than happy to be rid of me, axe murderer that I no doubt was.

The rain, which had increased in ferocity when I left my humble abode, had once again tapered off to a monotonous drizzle. I pulled out my flask, knocked back a suitable slug, then sidled over to the lighted entryway of the furniture store.

No Jerry. My watch said 12:10. Jerry had never been noted for his patience. Obviously he'd trudged on without me. Using a penlight flash, I checked the city map I'd brought with me. I'd been a Boy Scout in another lifetime. Be prepared. All I needed was a tent and a sleeping bag. Ethel Avenue was an extension of Ryding, so I headed down that forlorn street.

I'd seen ugly in my day, but the merry little promenade I found myself on now was major league. There was still a sweetish tinge to the air, only it wasn't really sweet; it was rank, as if something had slithered into the atmosphere and decomposed. Back in the old days it had been a lot worse, especially in the summer and when it wasn't raining. I had something to be thankful about.

It was too gloomy to see much as I ambled down the street, but I knew one of those super warehouse stores now occupied part of the site of the old stockyards. I could certainly recall the way it had once been: rusty oil drums, beetling buildings with turquoise siding, sun-bleached wooden corrals and chutes, railway tracks and more railway tracks, a riot of weeds, an obscene lushness of green. Abattoirs are like that. Blood does wonders for the complexion of chlorophyll. Without doubt the rust and greenery were still more vivid, more voluptuous here than anywhere else in the city. One time, when I was doing the series on meat-packers, I'd spotted a Judas heifer leading a tame herd across St. Clair Avenue to hamburger heaven. And for a few seconds I'd thought I'd been tossed back in time to Chaucer's England and would see, around the next corner, the smiler with a knife.

Despite the pitch-black, I could easily make out a few animal corrals still standing. The place was spooky. I could have used some cattle and porkers in those chutes. Empty, they looked ominous. Even a train roaring by would have been welcome. It was too quiet. All I could hear was the drizzle, both in my brain and without.

I looked up at the sky which, despite the rain, remained faintly orange. It was a big sky, and for a moment I thought I was on the prairies, an impression reinforced by a couple of derelict silos. And then I saw it. Harmony Meats. A few spotlights illuminated a billboard featuring an all-animal band. I particularly liked the goat on alto sax.

From across the narrow street I cased the joint. No cars, as far as I could see. No people. Just the Hot Five of Barnyard Jazz getting down to business in their electra-glide zoot suits. The building, what I could see of it, was the usual sick turquoise, a colour no doubt dictated by the avatars of abattoir aesthetics. The loading dock was on the left side of the building. A few lights were on there, so I figured that was as good a place to start as any.

I trotted across the street, passed through a gate in the open wire-mesh fence, and heaved my tired bones up. Cautiously I walked along the concrete dock, looking for an entrance. The roll-up mechanical doors were locked tight, but at the end of the dock I found an open conventional door. Wide open. Aiming my penflash at the abyss, I plunged in. The place had an old stink to it, of long-ago slaughter still redolent. A bit of paper on the floor caught my attention, and I stooped to pick it up. It was a candy wrapper. Chocolate mints. One of Jerry's favourite in-between-meals snacks.

The wrapper heartened me, but only for a moment. I was in a vast cavern of a place, almost totally devoid of light, stumbling toward I knew not what. The concrete floor was sticky and the air was close and foul. And all I could hear was incessant dripping, as if I'd been set adrift in a Tarkovsky film without a raft. Jerry would appreciate the celluloid allusion. If only I could find him.

As I edged forward, something slapped against my cheek, and I screamed. I really screamed. I jumped so high I lost my balance and tumbled into a heap on the slimy floor.

I lay there for a moment with my eyes closed tight, expecting some creature from the other side of beyond to tear a chunk out of me. Too many slice-and-dice flicks had fuelled my overripe imagination. But nothing happened.

While I tried desperately to reassemble my scrambled synapses and tamp down my rising gorge, I cocked an ear, straining to hear the slightest sound. But all I could pick up was the dripping and my own thudding heart.

"Jerry, are you there?" I croaked. When in doubt, reassure yourself with your own voice.

The dripping sounded closer. Almost right on top of me. And the concrete beneath wasn't just sticky; it was wet. There was water or something all over the floor. Or something. I crawled toward the loudest dripping and thrust out a hand. Nothing. Then something splashed on my fingers. Immediately I jerked the penflash up. Its weak, wavering beam caught something vaguely white, but I couldn't make out what it was. I moved closer and raised the flash higher.

"Jerry," I whispered, "say something."

The face floating above me was motionless, its mouth a great maw, its eyes popping. I screamed again and up-chucked bourbon and Jack's poi-poi. Then I heard a voice behind me, back where I'd entered the abattoir.

"Did you hear that?"

"A scream? Sort of strangled like?"

The first voice laughed. "You've been watching too many *Friday the 13ths*, Lupo."

I knew that raspy laugh, like sandpaper on a blackboard. Like a pick striking bone. It belonged to Nik Rorke.

"I tell you," the second voice insisted. "I heard a scream."

"You ever seen a pig butchered?" Rorke asked.

"Nope."

"Well, if you had, you'd know they don't scream after they're carved.

Besides, you're the one who did the carving. Didn't you make sure he was dead?"

"Yeah... sure," mumbled the second voice, obviously Lupo Vip's. "I still wanna turn on the lights for a minute."

"I don't want to hang around here, Vip. Believe me, it was a fuckin' rat or something. Did anyone you played with in Bosnia ever get up and walk away?"

"Lemme turn on the lights, anyway."

"Want to admire your handiwork, eh?" Rorke said. "Be my guest."

Without thinking, I scuttled away from the thing swinging above me. Like a tidal wave, panic flooded through my entire body. I had to hide. Now. Instantly. Groping the floor, my fingers nudged something metallic. An oil drum, and then another one, and a pile of tires. Frantically I pushed and pulled until I was pretty certain no one could see me. And then I was blinded. All of the lights in the abattoir came on at once.

Flashes. That's all I can remember. Two figures at the doorway, one short, one tall. One an unfinished abortion by a drug-crazed cartoonist, the other a new-wave assassin in mortician black, a .45 in human guise. And swinging on a meat hook in the middle of the big space, the object of their scrutiny, was the flayed carcass of Jerry Bauch, blood pooled on the concrete beneath his trussed feet. I looked at my hand and saw the blood, already dry, splattered there.

"Shame he didn't really know anything," Rorke said. "All mouth. But he's one little piggy who won't go oink again. Satisfied?"

"He ain't so little," Vip snorted, his gaze taking in the whole room, lingering on the pile of refuse that was my refuge. My heart stopped for a full beat, maybe two.

"C'mon, Lupo. Time to go."

"Yeah, yeah, okay. I'll turn off the lights."

"No. Leave 'em on. I kinda like the effect. Messages should always be as clear as day." I could have sworn Rorke looked straight at me.

The door banged shut and I heard an engine roar to life and then the skid of tires on gravel. They were gone. I looked at the hulk hanging on the hook. The darkness had been bad enough, but the glare of the cheap fluorescents was far worse. I tried to look away from the body, but couldn't. I was still looking when the cops came. I guess I had called them, but I couldn't remember how or when. By the time they got there, I was out of bourbon.

STATION XII

Perfect paralysis of the mind is hard to achieve. But after a couple of days of pickling myself with booze, I'd come pretty close to it, or a reasonable facsimile. The amazing thing was that Jerry was alive, even though Vip had banged up his head pretty good and had practised a little unorthodox liposuction on his body. The doctors said he was in a coma. They weren't sure he'd recover.

Jerry's family had decided to put on a prayer session at a non-denominational church that looked more like a crematorium. To my surprise, I joined the faithful. Obviously my private embalming needed work. The church was a concrete eyesore located in one of Toronto's many ravines, and as the mumbo-jumbo unfolded at the minimalist black-chrome-and-smoked-glass "altar" in front of me, I sized up the audience.

There weren't many people at the pseudo-Christian ceremony. Jerry's parents were there as well as his only sibling, a sister. Also in attendance were some colleagues from the *Globe*, a couple of friends, and a cadaverous yet oddly attractive woman who stood sniffling at the back of the room. I didn't know what religion Jerry had been raised in, if any. He certainly didn't practise anything that I knew of, and he never talked about anything personal, whether family or romance. He did talk incessantly about sex. It was one of his favourite subjects, along with food. But if he'd been involved with a woman or women more than casually during the years I'd known him, he'd never let on. He was more interested in other people's fuck-ups, though he'd soon grown bored of mine.

I looked back at the anorexic woman whose loud sniffs filled the room.

She had a vaguely Central Asian cast about her, maybe Bulgarian or Hungarian, and reminded me of numerous medieval paintings of women I'd seen over the years, particularly those by Cranach and Durer. Her tawny hair was impossibly, unfashionably long and straight, her cheeks unbelievably high, and her eyes incredibly sunken, with a trace of an epicanthic fold. "Rapunzel, Rapunzel, let down your hair," I whispered idiotically, wondering what connection the mysterious woman could possibly have with Jerry. Thinking about that made me realize how little I knew the man I considered my best friend. There were whole oceans of Jerry Bauch I'd never fathomed.

I did know that his parents were followers of some bland Christian cult, a kind of vague mélange of the United Church and EST. Jerry had once said that if they were going to return to religion in their old age, why couldn't they have at least had the decency to wrestle with snakes or sacrifice small children?

Jerry had never gotten along with his father and, looking at the man now, I could almost see why. The elder Bauch had Jerry's girth but not his height. If Jerry's substantial head reminded one of voluptuous visages from history, the elder Bauch's dead, doughy features bore a closer resemblance to Elmer Fudd. There was no fire, no gleam, not even a spark in that face. Jerry had once said that he could have hated his father with more clarity if the man had at least been a fanatic fundamentalist violently opposed to everything Jerry stood for. Instead, he'd been stuck with a fuzzy father who mildly disapproved of his son's career and behaviour. For a man of vast appetites and unbridled desires, a man like Jerry Bauch, the most heinous crime of all was sufficiency. Always perverse, Jerry despised his father for denying him the pleasure of pure, undiluted hate.

There was more to it than that, of course. There was Jerry's mother, perhaps the only person he really loved. No doubt Jerry held his father responsible for the crime of smothering his mother in the same banal ooze that swamped the old man's life.

But looking at Jerry's mother, a desiccated, bird-like creature with sharp, shifty eyes, I couldn't find any clue to her son's existence. No one says children have to bear any resemblance— physical, emotional, or intellectual— to their progenitors, but Jerry seemed entirely self-created. As for the sister, she was a perfect cookie-cutter copy of the father. Jerry had only mentioned her to me once, something about her being married to an insurance adjuster and living in Mississauga, as if that were crime enough on her part.

All of these thoughts unfurled in my brain as a screen against what I was really thinking. Jerry had almost been killed; in fact, he still wasn't out of the woods. He'd asked me to accompany him and I'd let him down— disastrously. But what was it that Rorke and Vip thought Jerry knew?

When the police had arrived on the scene, I'd gone at them like a crazy man, shouting at them, demanding they nail Rorke and Vip before it was too late. At the time I'd thought Jerry was dead, but by then I was more worried about myself. I was terrified the same thing would happen to me and overjoyed that I wasn't the one swinging on the meat hook.

Now, as I watched Jerry's father perform some kind of Masonic-like rite at the altar, my mind worked overtime on the mess things had become. Hell, I wasn't even really interested in *Cardenio*. All I cared about was Carole Rutland, and I didn't even know the real reason for that. Could Jerry have been tortured, almost killed, because of someone's misunderstanding of my curiosity about a lost crazy? Of course, there were several connections between Carole and *Cardenio*. But all three— Sharon Praeger, Donald Yates, and Garrett Macpherson— were dead.

Nik Rorke was the obvious heavy. Smart as he was, though, he was still only hired help. So I was left with one Satan behind the scenes— Cedric Shaw. But why would he kill off the people my curiosity had led me to? Could Avery Brownlee be the real puppet master?

I watched as Jerry's parents burned incense and started wailing incomprehensible incantations. Any minute, I thought, and they'd be drawing pentagrams on the floor and slitting the throat of a chicken. My head ached, and all I knew for sure was that I had to visit one place before going home— the liquor store. Jerry's parents had asked me to go with them to the hospital after the ceremony, but I couldn't. Hospitals did terrible things to me, and I needed to blot out the image of Jerry on the meat hook.

There had been a lot of private things I'd never known about Jerry; we didn't have that kind of friendship. But maybe we didn't have to swap details about the detritus of each other's life. We just *knew* each other. What did Montaigne say about why he loved his friend La Boétie? "Because it was he; because it was me," or something like that. Jerry was the best friend I'd ever had, except for maybe Jack Malone. And Jack, being older than I, made for a different equation. Then something occurred to me—Jack and Jerry were my only real friends— and I knew that all the alcohol in the LCBO wasn't going to fill the Marianas Trench that had opened up in my soul. I could almost feel Jerry sneering at his family's attempt at offering up prayers for his complete recovery, but I mumbled my own little plea for divine intervention.

As we filed out of the church and into the leaf-strewn ravine, I looked for the sad-eyed Tatar who had sobbed throughout the recondite ritual. But she had vanished. Just then a red-haired man in a lime-green seersucker sport coat and yellow double-knit polyester slacks grabbed my elbow and steered me toward the parking lot. My conductor was Peter Venable, better known as Peter Venal or Peter VD, a so-called commentator on Toronto's art scene for *CITY,* a weekly entertainment rag with counterculture pretensions.

"C'mon, Mickey, give me the scoop. Who tried to fillet ol' Jerry?"

Obviously Venable had attended the Ben Hecht school of journalistic dialogue. I brushed his hand away from my shiny navy blazer, checked my elbow for oil slicks, then turned to look at the guy. Venable's red hair was curly and tangled like a briar patch on fire. His ferrety face was twisted into what I imagined he thought was a grin, but all I could think of was a rat gnawing on its cage.

"If it isn't Peter VD," I said. "What's the matter, Petey? David Lynch not in town this week? I hear the mayor just had David Cronenberg's baby and she looks like the top of Sinéad O'Connor's head."

The rat no longer gnawed on his cage; now he wanted to chomp on me. "I'm a journalist, Mickey. You haven't forgotten what that means, have you? It's not every day a film critic gets hung on a meat hook."

Judging by the gleeful expression on Venable's pyrotechnical face, he was hoping a trend was in the making.

"I'm not in the mood, Venable. Go chase your story somewhere else."

"I hear your old friend Nik Rorke was involved."

Venable wasn't going to let me and my need for further numbness crawl away. The mere mention of Rorke's name jolted the paralysis I'd grown comfortable in.

"I know where you can find Rorke," Venable said slyly, his bright blue eyes pulsating like strobes, his merriment obvious at my distress.

"And how would a gossip columnist like you know something like that? Even the police haven't got a clue where he is."

"I have my sources," he said smugly.

"I'm sure you do." I eyed Venable carefully. What was going on? Was this another set-up? "Why haven't you told the police?"

"Are you kidding? The cops never tell me anything, and I'm a great believer in returning favours."

"So why tell me?"

"Bauch is your buddy. I figure you might like to know where to find the guy responsible for what happened to him. In exchange, you can give me all the gory details, and I do mean all."

We were standing beside a red Triumph, obviously Venable's car. I grabbed him by the lapels of his seersucker jacket and pushed him against the driver's door. "I've had a bad week, Petey. If you want bargains, go to Honest Ed's. Just tell me where Rorke is. Now!"

"Hey, watch the jacket, Finnegan."

Holding on to the *CITY* hack with one hand, I took out my key chain, selected a key, and dragged it along the side of the Triumph.

Venable wriggled like a lobster tossed into a pot of boiling water. "Fucking hell! Are you crazy?"

"Tell me, or I'm going to grace your car with my version of Picasso's *Guernica*."

Venable tried to break my hold, but all he could do was squirm some more. I was no heavyweight, but Venable was a weasel without fangs. He went limp. "Okay, stop! He's got a house in the Humber Valley near the marshes on the western side of the river."

"How about an address?"

"At the northern end of Stephen Drive. You can't miss it. It's the only house. Looks like a lodge up in Muskoka."

I looked closely at Venable. "You sound as if you've been there."

"I have."

"Really?" I tightened my grip.

"Shaw. The house belongs to Cedric Shaw. I did a piece about Shaw's store on Queen West a while back." Venable paused to catch his breath. "He told me he had some of his best stuff stashed at the Humber Valley place and invited me to see it. So I did. Rorke was there. It was pretty obvious he was living in the house."

"And the cops don't know about it?"

"I don't see how."

"How do you know Rorke's still there?"

"Guess you'll have to find out. Now tell me the juicy details about Jerry Bauch." Venable tried to grin. It was pretty hard to do with my hand rammed against his throat.

"The story's not finished yet." I let him go, and he fell to the gravel with a loud crunch.

"But... we made a deal."

"So sue me!" I yelled over my shoulder as I made my way out of the parking lot.

I didn't get far. A beaten-up black sedan of no apparent make pulled up beside me. Frank Kaplan stuck his head out the open window. "Need a lift?"

I nodded, went around to the other side of the car, and hopped in.

"What was all that about?" he asked, jerking a stubby thumb in the direction of Venable, who was picking himself up from the gravel.

I glanced at Kaplan but didn't say anything.

"Well?"

"Nothing. Just a couple of newsprint scribes comparing notes."

Kaplan considered that, then put the car into gear and drove out of the church's parking lot. "Where to?"

"Home, I guess." As we whipped out of the ravine in a swirl of leaves, I cocked an eye at the western sky. The sun, which had been pretty tentative all day, swooned along the horizon, as if mortally wounded by surging gusts of arctic wind. "I didn't see you at the ceremony."

Kaplan took a turn a little too sharply, then looked at me. "I was there. Outside. Watching."

"Still looking for *Cardenio,* eh?"

"Just like your friend, Mickey. Maybe you, too."

"I don't give a shit about that goddamn thing," I snapped.

Kaplan coughed. "I'm real sorry about your friend. We've got a uniform guarding his hospital room." The big cop drummed his fingers on the steering wheel. I didn't think he was capable of being embarrassed. When I remained silent, he cleared his throat again and said, "Yeah. Well, anyway, this might interest you. I found out these academic types have been analyzing anonymous plays with computers to find out who wrote them. It's called stylometry. It's all a lot of math to me. As far as I can guess, they tote up how many times a guy uses certain words. So I asked Brownlee if *Cardenio* had been checked that way. He said there wasn't enough time. Hell, they didn't even photocopy the bloody thing."

"Isn't there a computer project at U of T doing that sort of stuff?"

"Yeah, you bet. I checked it out. Talked to some of the brains. I thought maybe they could run a check on those last two lines in Macpherson's suicide note. You know, see if they are Shakespeare."

"And?"

"No luck. The computer whizzes say the sample's too small."

"Figures. From what I've heard, one computer ends up claiming Shakespeare couldn't have written most of *Macbeth* and another insists he wrote that godawful poem 'Shall I Die?' that someone dug up a few years ago."

"It doesn't matter, anyway," Kaplan said. "Remember that black gunk on Macpherson's hands?"

"Yeah."

"Well, our own lab boys did a chemical analysis, and it's ink, all right. The same stuff used in the suicide note. But the really interesting thing is what's in the ink." Keeping one eye on the road, Kaplan pulled a notepad out of his beige car coat pocket, flipped it open, and propped it on the dashboard. "That ink contains oak galls; copperas, a compound of copper and ferrous sulfate; gum arabic; logwood; vitriol; and traces of gun powder."

"What are oak galls?"

"That's what I asked. According to the lab boys, they're some kind of shit left by insect eggs on the leaves of oak trees."

"Pretty strange recipe for ink, isn't it?"

"Not if you're making the kind of ink they used in Shakespeare's time."

"Meaning Macpherson *was* into forgery?"

"Bingo. But there's more. We found a few gallons of this ink in Macpherson's house, plus a lot of other interesting stuff— goose quills and a ton of old paper, parchment and linen. It was down in his basement, along with all sorts of equipment— a nifty little oven for baking paper, work tables, a regular laboratory. He even had big vats, a press, and clothesline for drying paper, which Forensics tells me he used to size the linen paper. Seems the stuff has to be dunked into a hot solution of animal gelatin— leather shavings boiled in water— then smoothed out with a wooden mallet. And there were books, shelves of them. Handwriting manuals, histories of master forgers, recipes for ink, the whole nine yards. The only thing the guy didn't do was make his own paper. We figure he bought it somewhere."

"Any interesting video or audio tapes?"

Kaplan leered. It wasn't a pretty sight. "Yeah, you could say so. Seems our man was into porno as well as forgery. We found a whole mess of hard-core videotapes, not to mention some serious sex toys. Guy lived alone. Just him and his telegenic hunks."

"Macpherson was gay?"

"Might have swung both ways. We found a bunch of kiddie porn, too. Both sexes. We slogged through all of it. Nothing special, just the usual vomit."

I fidgeted with the knob on the glove compartment. "How about Carole? Did you find anything concerning her?"

Kaplan coughed. "Nope."

We were at the top of Avenue Road and about to tumble down what the locals called the "roller coaster." For a brief moment, before we plunged, I could see the glass-and-steel slabs of the city's financial district in all their gaudy glory. Like sassy tarts, they strutted alongside the concrete thrust of the CN Tower.

"So," I said, "Macpherson was a fraud and *Cardenio* is a hoax. I guess that'll make Eddie Fournier happy. Everything wrapped up neat and tidy. And the media will have a field day with the porn angle. Macpherson forged the manuscript, became a big academic superstar, then got cold feet and conveniently 'lost' the play. Of course, too many people knew— Sharon Praeger and Donald Yates, for example— so he had them bumped off, then had an attack of the guilts and did away with himself. Yeah, real neat. Only what about Jerry Bauch? Or Nik Rorke and Cedric Shaw? Or that little monster Lupo Vip? C'mon, Kaplan, whether *Cardenio* is a fake or Macpherson is a forger makes no goddamn difference at all."

"I never said it did. The whole thing stinks. But the official story is that Praeger was the victim of a psycho, maybe a Hammer Harry copycat. And Yates was the victim of some scam Cedric Shaw's into, maybe involving *Cardenio*."

"What about Jerry? Or doesn't he count in the Cartesian cosmos of criminology?"

Kaplan's foot got noticeably heavier on the gas, and we shot down the street a trifle too fast.

"Well?" I prompted.

"You're not going to like this."

"What's new? Spit it out, anyway."

"They think... well, maybe Bauch was... he got busted for drugs, you know."

"Goddamn it, Kaplan! That was years ago. Some piddling little cocaine possession charge."

"Yeah, well, the big problem with all this is that nothing makes sense if *Cardenio*'s a forgery. So the big boys think the play's a side issue. Shaw's into something else. Something big, like drugs."

"Christ almighty! Do you cops think everything boils down to drugs?

Let me guess. Jerry was smuggling Egyptian mummies impregnated with cocaine for Cedric Shaw. Or maybe shrunken heads stuffed with crack."

"They found a lot of coke in Bauch's apartment when they searched it, Mickey. And the tests show he had some in his system when Vip went to work on him."

"That's wonderful! So Macpherson's a sex maniac forger and Jerry's a dope-pushing drug fiend."

"Calm down, Mickey. It's not what I think."

"So what *do* you think?"

"I don't know. The thing's got me beat. We had Shaw down to headquarters for a real grilling, but we can't tag him with anything. And we can't find Rorke or Vip. This whole business is nothing but ghosts. Look at what we got. A play that's maybe fake but can't be found. A bunch of corpses that look like they're connected but nothing definite to prove it. And Jerry, who can't talk to us. Sure, someone's covering up something, but what? No university's going to touch that play with a ten-foot pole now. It's worthless."

"If it's a fake. If it isn't, it would still be priceless to a collector, some guy willing to pay big bucks for the pleasure of owning something Shakespeare wrote in his own hand, a play that's been lost for centuries."

Kaplan cast a quick look at me. "You want it to be real, don't you? The play, I mean."

"It's not what I want, Frank. It's the only thing that makes sense."

"So you figure Shaw set Macpherson up as a forger?"

"Something like that."

"How do we pin it on him?"

"Beats me, Sergeant."

Kaplan pulled the car up to the curb. We'd arrived at my apartment building. "Is there something you want to tell me, Mickey?"

I reached for the door handle, opened the door, and stepped out onto the sidewalk. Twisting around, I looked Kaplan in the eye. "Like what?"

"I wouldn't be asking if I knew."

"Thanks for the ride, Sergeant."

Kaplan rubbed his wide forehead, as if trying to fill in the deep fissures there. "Stay out of trouble, okay?"

I tried to grin, but it was a pathetic attempt. "The only trouble I intend to get into is a few hundred bottles of LCBO's finest."

Kaplan grunted, put the car into gear, and drove off. I stood there and watched until I couldn't see his car any more, then dashed into the building and down the stairs to my cave. Once inside, I changed into jeans and a red plaid flannel lumberjack shirt, put on some construction boots, and grabbed my windbreaker, a flashlight in case my quest took longer than I anticipated, and a city map. Before heading out the door, though, I called the hospital to see if there was any change in Jerry's condition. There wasn't, so, reinforced with anger, and more than a little guilt, I set out on my expedition.

It was crazy, and I knew it. I should have told Kaplan what Peter VD had told me about the house on the Humber. But I wanted to do this on my own. Demons faced, and all that. Kaplan had complained about too many ghosts in this whole goddamn business. He was right. They were my ghosts. Lately I'd developed the kiss of death in a big way. Hell, I was even a phantom myself, flitting around the edges of this great big fuck-up. It was time to act, to shake off two years of lethargy. Besides, there was still plenty of daylight, and even I could embark on a confrontation with a monster or two in the sun.

Of course, there was more. There always is. Since Kaplan had dropped the bomb about Jerry on me, I'd felt like throwing up. Jerry dirty? Jerry in league with the likes of Cedric Shaw and Nik Rorke? I couldn't believe it. Maybe the cops had endlessly Machiavellian minds seasoned by perpetual swimming through the sewers of a world-class city, but not me.

Jerry had had a drug habit once upon a time. I'd first met him in its last stages— the only time I'd ever known him to be vulnerable. I still remember the late-night call he'd made once in the grip of some heroin terror. He'd woken me up and I'd been less than sympathetic and a whole lot abrupt in my response.

Yeah, heroin. Jerry had been into just about every drug at one time or another. A true child of the sixties, even though he'd been a bit young to really be a part of the Woodstock generation. Both of us had come along at the ass end of the baby boomers.

I didn't tell Kaplan about Jerry's real drug past. It would have only made him more keen to see narcotics as the universal answer to the *Cardenio* conundrum. Anyway, Jerry had been clean for years. He'd been a great believer in experience, and the drug problem had been an experiment gone wrong. Jerry was no Coleridge, not even a Thomas De Quincey, just a guy, like thousands of others, who had thought he could handle anything. But Jerry a part of the malignancy that seemed to get blacker and fouler the more I probed? I'd never buy that.

Still, I couldn't be sure. Really sure. The answer lay in the house on the Humber. I had to go, even though every cell in my body was screaming, "No!"

The best way to get to my destination, according to my city map, seemed to be to drop down to Queen and catch the westbound streetcar to Stephen Drive where a bus would take me north practically to the front door of Shaw's secret house. Before I transferred onto the Queen car, I bought a meat patty from a street vendor. I hadn't eaten all day. The trip along Queen was uneventful. This was my second time out this way in a week. This time, though, I was going even farther west, right over the Humber River and into Etobicoke, a suburban wasteland I'd successfully avoided all the years I'd lived in Toronto.

The ride was long and monotonous. I'm not even sure I remember getting on the Stephen bus. And before I knew it, I was getting off the bus, just a stone's throw from the house where Nik Rorke was supposedly holed up.

All around me, as I walked down Stephen Drive, were small apartment buildings, mostly red brick. The neighbourhood was definitely suburban; it had the kind of buildings that had been thrown up in a hurry after the Second World War. The lawns and shrubs were neatly manicured, the trees, no longer suburban saplings, were carefully pruned, the streets scrubbed and swept; hell, even the leaves that should have been scattered everywhere had been done away with. The buildings themselves had an unreal aspect about them. They seemed to glitter in the waning sunlight, as if about to vanish in the blink of an eye. The street could have been a plaything of some Brobdingnagian child. But the owners were nowhere to be seen. In fact, there was no one anywhere. I had a hard time believing that anyone had ever lived in these buildings.

In the midst of all these pygmy highrises I couldn't feature the kind of house Venable had described. But as I approached the end of Stephen Drive, there it was— a largish fieldstone house with a many-gabled shake roof. It looked like a ski lodge plunked down in the middle of Toronto. Cedar balconies ran the length of the house and an intricate wrought-iron fence gave it the air of an estate, albeit a small one. There were two cars— a green Porsche and a white BMW— in the tiny slate-slabbed lot tucked to one side of the house. And a few lofty pines added to the seclusion of the place, which overlooked a bend in the sluggish Humber.

Cautiously I stepped over a chain marking the end of the asphalt street and the beginning of the gravel lot between the house and a bald, knobby hill carpeted in pine needles. Each step on the crunching gravel exploded in my feverish brain like a land mine. Turning away from the house, certain someone had heard me, I slowly edged over to the relatively steep slope. It was quite a view. Far below, besides the brown, brackish Humber, were dense marshes, a great many half-nude deciduous trees, and an incredible tangle of brush. An unholy silence lay over everything, perhaps augmented by the mist that clung to all the vegetation. Shaw had certainly picked a great site for his house. He got to look out at one of the last patches of wilderness left in the city.

Leaving the vista, I slid behind a dwarfish sycamore and shot a look at the house. Lights blazed in some of the windows. It was already getting dark. I'd have to duel with my dragons at night, after all. To make matters worse, the wind had risen and I could feel a storm brewing. In my bones, which were creaking loudly, I knew Nik Rorke was in there. And probably Lupo Vip, too. They were a team. Like Abbott and Costello, strychnine and Jonestown Kool-Aid, rape and pillage.

Standing there next to the shivering sycamore, I wondered what the hell I thought I was going to do. Storm the enemy citadel, guns ablazin'? Glide into the place like a cat burglar and karate-chop the inhabitants with kung-fu ferocity? Hell, I didn't have the faintest idea how to approach the house. And what was I really going to do if I did get in somehow? Bop Rorke with my flashlight?

I pulled the collar up on my windbreaker and clapped my arms around my chest to get warm. This entire escapade was insane. But maybe I could at least get a good enough look to see if Rorke was really in the house, then go call the cops and let the pros handle it. This St. George didn't have the stomach to slay any dragons tonight. Whatever bravado I'd had a couple of hours before had long since blown away with the wind. It would take nerve just to get closer to the house.

After eyeballing the place, I figured my best bet would be to get up on the low balcony where a lot of lights burned. I stood by the sycamore in quivering indecision for some time. It was pitch-dark. There was no moon, as far as I could tell, and if there were any stars, they were doing a good job of playing hide-and-seek. The river and marshes below were a big black void. The absolute darkness gave me the creeps, but I figured it was a good thing for what I was about to do.

Climbing carefully over the wrought-iron fence, which was more for decoration than security, I half crawled to the side of the house overhanging the valley slope, knocking loose stones into the jungle below. Some jewel thief I'd make, I thought, my heart doing a decent impression of a pinball tilt with every burst of noise.

Finally I was next to the balcony. The climb was easy, thanks to the rough stone of the house, and in a few seconds I was hoisting myself over the cedar railing, almost toppling into the spears of light lancing out of the floor-to-ceiling window. The horizontal blinds were open, so, my back against the bit of wall next to the window, I tried to peer into the room. The only thing I got doing that, though, was a crick in the neck. Then I heard the voices. Miraculously, the sliding window was slightly open, and I could hear what the people inside were saying quite clearly.

"What do you mean he wants me gone?" a voice with a proper British accent asked.

"Just what I said," another all-too-familiar voice answered. Nik Rorke's cemetery rasp was unmistakable.

"The police haven't got a thing on me," the first voice, Cedric Shaw's, protested petulantly. "They're running around in circles."

"Our friend doesn't want those circles to lead the cops to him," Rorke whispered coldly.

"Damn it, Rorke! You work for me, not him."

"Things change."

"You mean..."

"You got it, ol' chum. I'm a mercenary. I work for the guy with the biggest bankroll."

"Lupo," Shaw cried, "do something!"

"I work for Nik, Mr. Shaw," a third voice, Vip's, squeaked. "What he says goes."

"But I can't leave town. There are—"

"Who said anything about leaving town?"

"W-what? But you said he wanted me—"

"Lupo, grab his arm!"

"No... you can't..."

"Relax, Shaw, we're just gonna make you comfortable in the basement."

"You—"

I could hear scuffling, a few more panicky bleats from Shaw, a curse or two, then silence.

"Fuck!" Rorke muttered. "Now we have to carry the bastard. Get his feet, Lupo."

Chancing a peek, I saw Rorke and Vip lug the unconscious Shaw out of the room. Now was my chance. I spied a telephone on an ornate mahogany desk in one corner of the study, slipped through the window, and inched across the pile carpet as if treading on hot coals.

As I picked up the mock-Louis XIV receiver, intent on dialling 911, my eyes came to rest on the small teak bookcase behind the desk. It contained videotapes— no big deal— but one of the labels screamed out at me: Carole R! I put down the receiver and looked more closely at the bookcase. Each tape had a name on it: Theresa B, Christine T, Jacqueline S, Ingrid O, Maria M, Eva H, Lisa E, Penny L, Rita G, Sharon P. My eye lingered on the last one, but it was the Carole R tape that I pulled out.

"Christ, he was heavy," I heard a voice grumble. It was Rorke.

"We just gonna leave him down there?" Vip asked.

I tried to move, but I was frozen in place. I wasn't even sure if my heart was still pumping blood. With the Carole R tape still in my hand, I glanced at the telephone. There was no time to call the police. The voices were coming from the next room. I had to get out.

"Yeah," Rorke replied to Vip's question. "We're pulling out of here tonight. Who cares if the cops find him in the basement?" The hit man laughed, the sound of dry bones clacking. "What's he gonna tell 'em? Besides, the cops are already looking for us, so we'll just make ourselves scarce."

"I hate this town, anyway," Vip groused. "Montreal's the place to be."

"'Fess up, Lupo. You really miss Bosnia, don't you? Hey, maybe we'll check out Africa. Lots of fun there. C'mon, we better get moving. I'll start the car and you get the tapes."

My eyes popped, and the tape in my hand suddenly felt red-hot. I could hear footsteps approaching. Frantically I stuffed the tape into my windbreaker and headed for the window.

"Hey, you!" a voice cried out as I slipped onto the balcony. I didn't look back. The fat was in the fire, and so was I.

Without hesitating I catapulted myself off the balcony and into the gloom below, expecting a bullet in the head at any moment. When I hit the ground, I rolled in a tight ball right to the edge of the steep slope to the river. Then, adrenaline surging through my veins, I scrabbled downward, my clothes catching on brambles, pine needles stinging my face.

Behind me I could hear incoherent shouts and a great deal of crashing about. I didn't know where I was going. I was operating on pure animal instinct. Flight mattered. About halfway down I lost my footing, started tumbling head over heels, and didn't stop until I splashed into something.

Had I reached the river? Thrashing around, I tried to stand, but slid into muck. I was up to my calves in swamp.

"D'you see him?" a voice bellowed somewhere behind me.

"See him? Fuck, I can't see my own goddamn nose!" another voice yelled.

They were right behind me. On hands and knees I crawled through the slime, afraid that if I stood and fell again, they'd hear me. Sharp rocks tore at my flesh and many-legged things skittered across my knuckles, but I didn't care. I had to get away.

"He's over there!" a voice, Rorke's, I thought, cried. "I can hear him."

"Nah," Vip said. "That's a raccoon or something. He's headed the other way— toward the lake."

I had no idea which way I was going, but I had to get to my feet and run for it if I wanted to live. Straightening, I propelled myself forward and staggered on. I was trodding more solid ground now, and my eyes had adjusted to the darkness. I looked up at the sky, vainly hoping for some clue indicating my direction. Then, for the first time since plunging down the hill, I turned and spotted Shaw's house floating high above, ablaze with light.

I had my bearings. Vip was right: I was heading southward to the lake. Eventually I'd get out of this marsh and find the river proper. Maybe I could lose my pursuers that way; they'd figure I'd try to get to the nearest street rather than continue to follow the river. And, besides, the trees and bushes provided cover. Then a horrible thought occurred to me: what if there were bottomless bogs out there? I had no idea, but there were no other alternatives.

That was all the rational thought I had for some time. When I heard what sounded like stampeding buffalo behind me, I bolted, clawing my way through the vegetation, ripping, stomping, slashing, windmilling through the dark tangle, every step difficult as the spongy ground sucked at my boots, threatening to swallow me whole. If the homicidal bloodhounds on my trail had been uncertain about my whereabouts before, they certainly weren't now. But I figured Rorke and Vip were just as overwhelmed by this overgrown thicket as I was.

I became a frenzied dervish, a maddened juggernaut flailing through the flora as if on fire. Eventually I hacked my way out of the cattails and reeds and into a flat, grassy expanse. I was quite close to the narrower river and felt terribly exposed. Not looking back, I tottered on.

I could see better, thanks to the occasional light pole. An asphalt pathway skirted the river, and I followed it. On my right was a high concrete wall topped by a wire-mesh fence. The place looked like a penitentiary. Then my nostrils were bludgeoned by the stench, and I knew what it was— a sewage treatment plant.

My chest felt like a smelter, and little trucks were dumping landfill in my throat, but I pounded over the pathway even faster, only coming to a halt when I heard something splash in the reeds on my left. I spun around, and in the half-light I saw an enormous blue crane launch itself skyward. I stood there transfixed, then remembered what was behind me. This was no time for birdwatching.

I could hear the cars now, whipping along the Gardiner Expressway, and as I stumbled forward, my lungs ready to supernova, I spotted a tremendous array of light ahead. Stairways led to the streets above, but I was still afraid to show myself. The river, little more than a sewer at this point, slid beneath its concrete girdle to the lake beyond. I picked up a plastic bag lying on the ground, wrapped the videotape in it, and made sure the package was secure in my jacket. Then, holding my breath, I slipped into the murk and dog-paddled under the thundering expressway and railway tracks, feeling a powerful tug as I surged into the lake proper. I was a lousy swimmer, and the undertow was pulling me farther out. Panic-stricken, I pummelled the water, trying to get closer to shore. Then I could feel the bottom and slogged forward, eventually reaching a scrap of sand, easily the sorriest excuse for a beach in the universe.

Somehow I flung myself onto the shore, flopping into the oily debris in total exhaustion. I couldn't move another inch. If Lake Ontario's toxic cocktail didn't kill me, the unexpected steeplechase I'd just run would.

I looked up at the sky. Dawn was approaching. Off to the east I could see the sun's first shafts streak the horizon. Ahead of me the immensity of the lake spread southward, seemingly endless. If I really concentrated, shutting out the traffic noises, not looking right or left, only directly ahead, I could almost imagine what the lake might have been before the mammoth Panasonic billboard, the highrise toadstools, the belching factories, the ribbons of asphalt.

Lying on my back, my weight supported by my elbows, I was no longer in Toronto but with Laura in Pukaskwa National Park on Lake Superior. We'd gone up there for a week in the summer, one glorious week in total isolation. Pukaskwa was a wilderness park— no roads, no towns, about as off the beaten track as you could get. The only access was by plane, canoe, or foot. We'd hiked and canoed in from Heron Bay, and we'd discovered how much had been lost in the rest of the country.

When we camped on the lakeshore, our only companions the cry of loons, the howl of wolves, and the sigh of the wind in the boundless dark of evergreens behind us, Laura and I had sprawled out on a great slab of pink granite jutting into the frigid water. Our world was reduced to a jet-black dome dusted with fairy silver, the hard, ancient rock beneath us, and the big lake stretching into infinity. Arm in arm, we'd tried to identify the constellations. Laura was terrible at it, and I wasn't much better, so we'd invented our own. On either side of our perch was the beach, a swath of pebbles like no other I'd ever seen. This was a beach for titans, for gods. Its gleaming was limitless, pristine, primeval, the only sign of humanity the many pictographs Laura and I had found etched into the rocks rimming the water.

We'd made love, Laura and I, on that granite table, our limbs entangled, our nude bodies shivering, our swollen flesh smacking as we'd come together under the stars. Then, breathless, spent, we'd lain close, Laura poking and prodding my skin as she always did, as if looking for something she could never find, while I absently fingered her tawny hair and stared at the moon, wishing things could always be this way, knowing the cracks had already developed, knowing some day, perhaps soon, I'd lose her forever.

Now, sprawled on the soiled strip of Lake Ontario beach, I cried, great wracking sobs that blotted out the lapping of the water near my toes. Soaked to the skin, mud-caked, clothes torn, body bruised, I curled up and hugged myself. A ball of fire rose in the east and shot tentative spears across the dirty sky. Closing one eye, I caught sight of the blinking CN Tower, its soaring shaft rammed hard into the dawn. I was back in Toronto, with a vengeance.

STATION XIII

It was very bright. I was on a vast plain broken only by the limitless thrust of a slender tower some distance away. The hard white sand beneath my feet sent up waves of heat that penetrated every cell in my body. The landscape thrummed with the brilliance of the furnace blazing in the burnt blue sky. I blinked. There were no shadows. Everything was sharply defined. I was afraid that if I moved I would cut myself on this strange world of deadly clarity.

Then I spotted them. At the base of the plinth-like structure stood a motley group of figures. I moved forward, and even though I had only taken one step, I found myself in the midst of the crowd milling around the tower.

"We've been waiting for you," said one of the figures, who was dressed in a helmet, chain mail, leather jerkin, and leggings, and carried a shield and a short sword. The shield had a cross on it.

"Only you can do it," said another. This one wore a golden helmet, a white plume, a golden breastplate, and a white linen tunic.

"We've tried everything," a wild-looking fellow in rags wailed. "Luscinda is lost!"

"I keep tellin' you, Cardy," a man in a buff trench coat and forties-style hat snarled, "her name's Linda Loring."

"Eurydice, Eurydice, don't despair," piped up a guy in a knee-length snow-white tunic cinched with a gold cord. He was holding a lyre.

"Whatever you do, Orph, don't start that shriekin' you call singin' again," cracked the wise guy in the trench coat.

"We must do something," said a handsome youth in a blue tunic. He had a small harp slung over one shoulder and a bow and quiver of arrows over the other. With a string bass, a drum kit, and a horn or two, I figured this bunch might have the makings of a band. "If we do not act immediately, we will lose Isolde to King Mark forever."

"Whoa, Tristy, slow down," snapped Trench Coat. "You sure that love potion you knocked back wasn't bourbon? Let's get one thing straight. The geezer up there is Mendy Menendez and he's got his mitts on Linda."

Trench Coat glowered at the frantic crew around him, daring anyone to contradict him.

They were quiet for a moment, then the first guy, the one in chain mail and leather, swished his sword around and smiled wanly at Trench Coat. "My dear Philip, you seem to think this is a joke. You know as well as I do that Guinevere is the object of our quest."

"Linda Loring," growled Trench Coat.

"Luscinda!" bawled the crazy guy in rags.

"Eurydice!" cried Orphy.

"Isolde," groaned Tristy.

"Ariadne!" roared the pretty one in the gold helmet.

"Stop it!" an emaciated bag of bones wheezed. I hadn't seen this one before. He wobbled into the crowd of frenzied lunatics, halted in front of the tower, tottered dangerously for a moment, then pulled himself erect. The guy wore a brass barber's bowl tied to his head with green ribbons. The rest of his outfit featured a black, mouldy breastplate streaked with rust, a dirty, patched doublet, and tattered green leggings. In one hand he clutched a trash-can lid and under the other arm he carried what might have been a broken lance or perhaps a table leg. When I looked closely at the old-timer's face, all I could see were bad teeth, an enormous hairy mole, a hooked nose, dark craters where the eyes should have been, and an immense, drooping black moustache displaying evidence of a week's worth of dinners. For some reason the guy had a half-dozen wineskins slung around his spindly body.

"Señors, señors," the apparition pleaded, "we all know the object of our attention is the exquisitely beautiful Dulcinea. But—"

"In a pig's eye," rasped Trench Coat, spitting tobacco juice on the ground.

The old geezer gathered himself to his full height, which wasn't much, rattling the curious collection of metal utensils hanging from his belt in the process. "Señor Marlowe, I assure you Dulcinea is not a pig's ass. And I warn you, if you insult her once more I shall be forced to shed blood."

"In—"

"Enough," the old geezer croaked. "We must set aside our petty differences. We have tried everything to rescue the fair damsel imprisoned in the castle by that wicked giant Pandafilando the Squinter, and we have failed miserably. But now we have reinforcements, and it is to him that we must turn."

Every eye looked at me as if I had all the answers. I glanced up at the tower, which was made of glass. There was a small opening high up, but no other way, that I could see, to get in. Farther up, at the top, I could make out two figures. One of them had long hair. The other was no giant, but he looked mean, decked out in black the way he was. No, I thought, it can't be Nik Rorke. No way. Not here.

"Well, sweetheart," Trench Coat lisped, curling his lip, "we ain't got all day."

"Philip Marlowe would never say 'ain't,' and he wouldn't spit tobacco juice," I objected.

"Jeez, a critic! Well, you ain't no Raymond Chandler, either, bub."

"Enough, enough! We must act!" the guy in the gold helmet trumpeted. "Our ladders are too short to reach the opening in the tower. What must we do?"

I squinted up at the window again, then over at my personal band of Keystone Kops. "You guys look pretty strong." I eyed the old geezer narrowly. "Most of you, anyway. We'll make a human ladder. C'mon." I waved at Gold Helmet. "What's your name?"

"Theseus."

"Should have guessed. Okay, you'll be the base." I positioned him against the tower. "You next, Lance." The guy in chain mail climbed up on top of Theseus's broad shoulders. Soon the rest of them were in place, forming a wobbly pillar of noble flesh.

"What about me?" the old geezer squeaked plaintively.

"You'll supervise, Gramps," I said. "Make sure I don't put my foot on somebody's nose."

"Hey, Pops," Trench Coat yelled down, "got any booze in those wineskins?"

The old geezer scowled and made an obscene gesture. Then, shaking my head, I began to climb the human ladder. Finally I reached the top, hefted myself onto the not-so-beefy shoulders of Cardenio, and tried not to look down. As I straightened, the guys below me started to shudder. I figured any moment they'd collapse and we'd all land on Gramps, squashing him as flat as the surrounding landscape.

There wasn't much time. Carefully I stretched out my arms. I could just reach the window. I wasn't a strong guy, so how was I going to hoist myself up and through?

"H-hurry," Cardenio quavered beneath me. "C-can't hold... on much—"

I jumped, grabbed at the windowsill, and somehow hauled myself up into the opening. Then I heard a jumble of curses and the thud of many bodies smacking the sand. Looking down, I saw a dusty human heap at the base of the tower. Luckily Gramps had managed to scamper out of the way in time. He was dancing, rather sprightly, around the muddle of tangled limbs.

"You guys all right?" I called down.

They started to get to their feet and dusted themselves off.

"Do not worry about us!" cried Gramps. "Behead the giant!"

"Nix to Mcndy!"

"Slay the Minotaur!"

"Defeat Don Fernando!"

"Conquer King Mark!"

"Annihilate Hades!"

"Vanquish Modred!"

"Do it for all of us," Gramps grated, his raspy voice near the breaking point. "Do it for your own love. There is no turning back."

I saluted, and they cheered. Then I turned and took stock of where I was. In the gloom I could pick out stairs spiralling upward. Wonderful, I thought, no elevators. Sighing, the guys' cheers still in my ears, I pushed forward and began climbing the stairs.

At first I took them two or three at a time, but soon, out of breath, my heart doing a drum solo, I was down to one at a time, and that just barely. My own love, I thought as I wheezed up the seemingly endless spiral. Who could that be? Laura? Carole Rutland? No, I hardly knew her. Then who? More to the point, who was the guy in black? Even more to the point, where the hell was I and how did I get here? The last thing I remembered I was lying half-dead on a pile of oily sand on Lake Ontario.

Pretty soon, though, all I could think of were the stairs. I gave up counting them after I hit two hundred. Then, when my lungs felt as if they were giving my brain a bear hug, I saw a dim light. I was almost at the top.

Somehow I found new strength and catapulted my leaden body up the remaining steps until I stood on a platform open to the sky, black now, lit only by stars and a full moon. Frantically I looked around. And then I saw them. The moonlight shone on the woman's blonde hair, causing it to gleam like polished silver. Her alabaster gown shone like a beacon in the surrounding gloom. The black-garbed fellow stood beside her. He had a huge black cape furled around his body. The couple were holding hands rather tenderly.

Limping, thanks to the spasms in my tortured legs, I stumbled toward the pair, and as I reached them, they turned. My gaze flickered to the woman first, then to the man, but as my brain started to register their features, a flash of silver cut in front of my face, heading for my neck, and I screamed and screamed and screamed and screamed...

"Mickey, wake up! It's all right," a lovely voice insisted next to my ear.

"Wh-what the hell?" I groaned, falling halfway off my burnt orange living room couch.

"You're all right now," the voice repeated.

I blinked, rubbed my eyes, and squinted into the face of an angel. It was Brigit Malone. "Some dream," I muttered.

"I bet," Brigit said, bathing me in her king-sized smile. She was kneeling next to the couch. Besides the smile, she wore a white linen jacket and long skirt and a white silk blouse. A floppy white linen hat rode the swirl of her marvellous blonde hair and a crimson silk scarf splashed around her lovely long neck.

"H-how did you get in?" I asked, trying to boot the cotton batting out of my head.

Brigit sat on the couch beside me, concern creasing her radiance. "Your door was ajar. I heard you crying out. I thought something horrible was happening to you."

I coughed, but the cobwebs stayed.

Brigit frowned. "What kind of nightmare were you having?" Waves of compassion swept over me, a veritable deluge of empathy.

I looked away. "You don't want to know."

"That bad, eh?"

"It was ludicrous and terrifying at the same time." I grinned at her. "You going to psychoanalyze me, Herr Doktor?"

Brigit's usually lively emerald eyes got that smoky soulfulness that always puzzled me, a look that suggested deep, irredeemable anguish. They almost seemed to disappear beneath her thick tawny eyebrows. Then her ripe but not pouty lips rippled into the slightly skewed smile that I think knocked me out even more than her megawatt, full-blast version. "I'm not a psychologist yet, Mickey. I probably never will be." As soon as she said *never,* her features clouded again.

"You don't know that."

With one hand she pushed her hair away from her head as if it offended her, then whispered, "Oh, yes, I do."

The conversation seemed to be heading in the same direction as our last one when I'd been over for supper at her place, so I decided a new tack was in order. "What brings you over here? You've got a big heart, but even you couldn't hear me yelling all the way over where you live."

She flashed me a smile again. "No. I came to deliver a message. I could have phoned, but..."

"In person would be better?"

"Yes, exactly. Uh, the message. Jack told me you can meet him over at a friend's place tonight and play your videotape."

"Tape?" I wondered out loud. "Oh, yeah, right."

I'd called Jack when I stumbled into my apartment some time after eight in the morning. After my adventure in the Humber Valley, I'd fitfully slept for a while on the beach. When I woke up, I'd somehow gotten a cab home. Once inside my cave, all I'd wanted to do was crawl into a dark corner somewhere and obliterate myself. Before collapsing on my couch I'd tipped off the cops anonymously about what had gone down in the Humber Valley the previous night. But first I'd called Jack, since he had a VCR, one of the many technological marvels I had yet to acquire. I wanted to see the tape myself before handing it over to the cops. But all I got at Jack's end of the line was his answering machine, which reminded me...

"Why didn't Jack just call and leave a message on my machine?" I asked.

"He tried, but the phone just kept ringing."

I looked over at the telephone. The cord wasn't plugged into the jack. "Christ, I must have really been whacked. Didn't close my door and somehow knocked the phone cord loose."

Brigit crinkled her pert nose. "Just what *have* you been doing?" Her eyes were aimed at my shirt.

I looked at my clothes sheepishly. My Lake Ontario diving duds. "Pretty bad, eh? Let's just say I've been moonlighting in septic tanks."

"Anyway, I was away most of the day myself. Conor needed to get some shots at the clinic and I had errands. This is a really busy time for Jack, what with faculty meetings, classes, and so on. And now he's gotten himself involved in a new symposium on William Blake. That's what the meeting tonight's about. You could still come over to our place and play—"

"Uh, no," I said quickly. "I think—"

"But our VCR's broken. It was fine a couple of nights ago when Jack and I watched a movie."

I rubbed the side of my head absently. "Well, maybe I can find another one somewhere."

"No, Jack insists you go over to this colleague's place. He says it's all right. The man— Bob Berton's his name— has a big house and you can play whatever it is you want to play in privacy."

"Jack doesn't mind? I won't get in the way of his meeting?"

"Absolutely not." Brigit rummaged through her straw-coloured shoulder bag and extracted a piece of paper. "Here's Bob's address. Jack will be there at eight tonight and you can go over any time after that."

I took the piece of paper. The address was 1 Austin Terrace.

"Bob lives up near Casa Loma. He's in the fine arts department."

I put the scrap of paper in my shirt pocket. I wasn't too crazy about viewing the tape at a stranger's place, but I did want to see it tonight and maybe it would be a good idea to have Jack see it with me. I needed to talk to someone about this whole mess.

"Mickey," Brigit said, breaking into my thoughts, "what's this all about? I mean, what's so important about this videotape?"

"It has something to do with Carole Rutland's disappearance. And maybe *Cardenio,* too."

Brigit was fidgeting with her hat and biting her lip.

"Are you okay?" I asked her.

"It's too bad about Carole, isn't it, Mickey? She was very young, and pretty."

My eyebrows were about to enter the stratosphere. "You met Carole?"

"Did I say I met her?"

"Not in so many words." I looked at Brigit's slender hands. "If you don't watch it with that hat, it'll need life support."

Her fingers, which had nearly squeezed the linen hat into a chamois, jerked as if jolted with electricity. "I don't think I ever met her." She fell silent and studied the shell hole my couch cushion had become. "Jack, though, he knew her, didn't he?"

"Some time ago, sure. She took one of his creative writing courses. But then you know that."

Her poor hat discarded, Brigit's fingers were now probing the moonscape of my couch. At least she couldn't do any damage there. "Yes, I know that."

"Brigit, are you trying to tell me something?"

Her fingers ceased rolfing the cushion. Then she looked up suddenly. Her face spoke of tombstones and tragedy. "Mickey has... Jack... has Jack ever mentioned his... ?"

"His what?"

She glanced away, her eyes resting on one of my bookcases. "Nothing— oh, I don't know. I'm worried, that's all."

"C'mon, Brigit, what is it?"

Rather than answer, she cocked her head sideways. "*Women Beware Women,* what's that about?"

I looked at the bookcase. Obviously we were changing subjects, or were we? "It's a Jacobean revenge tragedy filled with the usual depraved monsters and slaughtered innocents. Brigit—"

She picked up a pen that was lying on the end table and began doodling on a pile of newspapers stacked on the arm of the couch. "Jack's distracted these days."

"He is pretty busy."

"Busy. Yes, busy Jack. All work and no play." She laughed harshly and stopped scribbling. "I've got to go, Mickey. Conor is waiting for me at pre-school." She stood, retrieved her hat, and stuck it on her head. "If Jack calls, can I tell him you'll see him at Bob's?"

"Sure," I said, hoisting myself off the couch. I escorted her out of my apartment and up to the building's front door.

Brigit hovered in the doorway. We were very close, almost touching. Her face flushed and her eyes moistened. For a moment I thought she was going to cry. Nervously her right hand flew to her neck and then dropped to her side.

"What is it?" I whispered.

She shivered slightly, then kissed me full on the lips and almost sagged against me. Instinctively I raised my arms to hold her, but she straightened with new resolution. "Conor is so impatient. I'd better run." A moment later she was gone.

Shaking my head, I returned to my apartment. I'd never seen Brigit so upset except when she was revealing her tortured childhood. Jack and Brigit had had their problems in the past; they'd even separated for a while before Conor was born. I wasn't too keen on viewing the videotape in a strange house, but I was even more determined to talk to Jack tonight.

My watch said it was just after five o'clock. Time enough to take a shower, get a bite to eat, and read the newspaper. I figured Cedric Shaw's corpse must have been discovered by now.

After cleaning myself up and changing into a pair of grey cords and a blue denim shirt, I plunked down on the couch and pulled on my loafers. Sitting there, I noticed Brigit's arabesques on the newspaper. They gave me a chill. Amid all the meaningless flourishes she'd written: "Women Beware Women. Women Beware Men. Men Beware Women. Beware Thyself. They'll never find her."

Never find her? I thought. Carole Rutland? Or was Brigit referring to herself? I didn't know what to make of her newsprint runes. Maybe they were just the idle nonsense of someone extremely agitated. But what was the cause of her anxiety?

At that moment my already roiling stomach gurgled with new ferocity, so I pulled a battered brown leather jacket out of the closet, left my apartment, and trotted over to the neighbourhood greasy spoon, an all-night dive that served food fit for the undead. After I ordered the twenty-four-hour breakfast special, the safest thing on the menu, I settled into a cracked vinyl booth the colour of French-Canadian pea soup and began to read the *Toronto Star* I'd bought on my way to the diner.

Hacking my way through the dense newsprint jungles of ads, human interest stories, hard news, and the daily detritus of yet another day in the world-class metropolis, I got increasingly frustrated. Finally my ham and scrambled eggs arrived and I dug into it as if it were the last meal I'd ever see. When I was finished, I got a coffee refill and dived into the newsprint once more. But there was nothing about Cedric Shaw. I knew I should call Frank Kaplan, but I was afraid he'd ask me too many questions. Still, I had to tell him about Rorke and Vip.

Sighing, I paid my bill and went over to a pay phone near the entrance to the restaurant. After I punched in Kaplan's number, the phone rang for a while, then a voice answered, "Fifty-two Division. Henderson speaking."

"Uh," I blurted.

"Hello?"

"Uh, is Sergeant Kaplan there?"

"Frank's out. Can I take a message?"

I hesitated, wondering if I should get Kaplan to meet me at Jack's friend's place. Then I decided I'd watch the tape first and call him later. "Will he be back?" I asked.

"Yeah, I think so. He's on duty all night."

"Thanks. I'll call back." I hung up and looked at my watch. Time to get moving. My stomach felt like Belfast on a bad night, so I figured I'd work off the Valvoline coffee and Play-Doh ham and eggs by walking up to Jack's friend's house. The Casa Loma area wasn't far, but it was mostly uphill. If nothing else, I'd get a workout.

The lowland part of the journey skirted the city streetcar yard, crossed the CPR tracks, and threaded through a grimy stretch of shabby red brick factories, scruffy car body shops, and a repugnant college campus that seemed to be an architectural paean to industrial oppression, sort of Chernobyl as ancient Greek Athenaeum. When I hit the corner of Davenport and Walmer, I started ascending one of the city's few geological prominences, the ridge that marked the shoreline of the prehistoric Lake Iroquois.

Where once mastodons gazed out over the glacial mega-sea that inundated present-day Toronto, the city's moneybags had practised one-upmanship by erecting monumental mansions to their own vanity. But when it came to Casa Loma it was game over. No one else had had the balls or the balminess to build another fairy-tale bastion on the bluff. Spawned before World War I but never really finished, the castle might have been dreamed up by Sir Walter Scott after a visit to an opium den. Instead it was the crazy brainchild of Sir Henry Mill Pellatt, a Toronto millionaire who made his bucks by lighting up the province with the early twentieth century's invisible gold— hydro-electricity.

As I huffed and puffed up the steep incline of Walmer, I hugged the massive stone wall marking the western boundary of Pellatt's one-time estate, marvelling over the kiss Brigit had given me before she'd taken a powder. Jack didn't know how good he had it. If he was screwing around again... But I didn't want to wrestle with that. I was an innocent bystander. What really had me scratching my head was Brigit's implication that Jack and Carole Rutland had had something going. But that was crazy. Jack had always let me in on his escapades. I couldn't see him hiding an affair with Carole, given my interest in finding her.

Finally I reached the top of Walmer where it swooped into Austin Terrace, and none too soon. The overbearing gloominess of Casa Loma's fieldstone walls and the tangle of deciduous trees overhanging them were beginning to get to me. My first glimpse of the facade of Pellatt's folly was, as always, exhilarating. Partially illuminated, it was difficult to tell that the gargantuan edifice was something of an illusion, tricked out as it was with a sandstone facing over a concrete shell. The eye was too busy flitting from tower to terrace to turret. As I strolled slowly down Austin Terrace, I had a hard time prying my attention away from the bristling battlements spread out before me. The grey-and-buff confection sailed out of a dream into the cool satin surrounding it.

By the time I shook myself out of the trance, I was standing at the gates to the estate. I consulted the slip of paper with Jack's friend's address— 1 Austin Terrace. Casa Loma took up one side of the street all by itself. Across from the castle was a row of pygmy mock-Tudor houses. Bob Berton obviously lived in one of those.

There wasn't much light, so I nervously crossed the street to get a better look at the numbers; Walmer made a blind curve into Austin Terrace, and I'd long had a certain knowledge that if I died prematurely, it would be on the bumper of a speeding maniac barrelling around a corner. But since arriving at Casa Loma, I hadn't seen one car. In fact, the whole neighbour-hood was unnaturally quiet. No barking dogs, no wind in the semi-nude trees or telephone wires, no echoing footsteps, no sirens, none of the usual big-city cacophony.

I had to get up really close to the first mock-Tudor house. Like its companion, it was totally dark, as if no one lived there. When I finally located the tiny scuffed brass address number, it read 20. Moving to the next house, I spied 18. If this side of the street was even, then the other side was... But how could that be? Casa Loma took up all of Austin Terrace on that side.

Turning around, I carefully scanned the immense concrete pile. I'd never been in Casa Loma, but I knew the Kiwanis Club ran it as a museum. What was going on? Had Brigit made a mistake in the address?

I peered into the gloom in both directions, then gingerly crossed the street again and walked through the open gates of the estate. As I approached the ornate porte cochere at the main entrance to the loopy palace, the light improved, but there wasn't much to see unless you figured parking lots were exciting.

While I stood there contemplating my next move, I heard a loud crash reverberate from somewhere inside the make-believe castle. Without thinking, I tried to budge the big baronial wooden door, but it was locked tight. Then, moving out from under the porte cochere, I spied a side door to the left, but when I tried to pry it open, it, too, was uncooperative.

Frustrated, I circled the building and found the gate to the rear garden wide open. As I slipped through, floodlights here and there cast a weird glow over the tangle of shrubs and flowers. My nerves were so frazzled that the crunch of gravel underfoot sounded like gunfire. Ahead I could make out a large object, then I heard the peal of a gong-like bell, although it could have been a grenade exploding, judging by how far I jumped. Edging closer, I glimpsed what looked like a metal dragon atop a tree of bells. Maybe it was a wind chime of some kind. But there wasn't much wind and the bells appeared to be the type that had to be struck if you wanted any noise.

Frantically I looked around, expecting someone to leap out of the bushes. But when no Freddies or Jasons or Hammer Harrys pirouetted out of the forsythia, I leaned over and squinted at the sign attached to the dragon sculpture. It spoke of pure hearts ringing bells and awakening beneficent dragons that would bring hope, love, peace, health, wisdom, and other goodies. Not my kind of dragons, I thought. Where I came from, dragons weren't so nice.

As I straightened, something banged heavily to my left, toward the house. Inhaling, I trudged on in the direction of the noises, passing beneath an archway entwined with vegetation. My skin prickled with anticipation, and sweat trickled down my clammy sides. What in hell was I doing here? Every muscle in my rapidly perspiring body was knotted tightly, waiting for a downpour of blows. But I got through the archway unscathed and found myself standing on the lower terrace next to a cannon, the kind the British once tied rebellious Sepoys to prior to blowing them to kingdom come.

Looking toward the upper terrace of Pellatt's delusion, I spotted what was causing the racket. One of the French doors leading inside was ajar, and the rising wind did the rest. As I got closer, I saw something big and dark sprawled near the door. Reluctantly I stooped to get a better look. The man seemed to be wearing a uniform. I didn't have a whole lot of experience with dead people, although lately that had been changing, but the guy didn't look as if he was ever going to get up again. He was lying on his face, and when I turned him over, there was an awful lot of blood oozing from his chest.

There was another body on the other side of the door. Straightening, I climbed over the dead security guard and entered the house. Slumped on the wooden floor of what appeared to be, even in the gloom, a huge room, was a tiny mole of a man. Near the second body was a flashlight, which I snatched up and flicked on. The pale light picked out the unmistakable features of Lupo Vip. The bullet hole in his forehead didn't do anything for the hit man's goofy grotesqueness.

Had the security guard and Vip struggled, only to kill each other? That's what it looked like. But Nik Rorke couldn't be too far away, and that thought made my skin crawl.

I didn't get any time to grapple with all this new information. Someone was on the stairs leading to the second floor. Loud creaking told me that much. Now was the time to go and get reinforcements. Two dead bodies were too much for me, and I sure as hell didn't want to make a third personally. But I'd come this far, so I picked up the gun that had supposedly done all the damage to Vip and the guard. It was a neat little chrome pistol, which I assumed belonged to Vip, since guards didn't usually carry guns.

I'd done some security guard work myself after the Diane Davis fiasco. But guns were alien to me. I had only a vague idea how to shoot, largely garnered from TV cop shows. For all I knew, there were no bullets left in the magazine. At least I could be certain the safety was off. I doubted either of the recently deceased had had the presence of mind to snick it back on.

Gun in hand, the flashlight gripped in my other fist, I headed for the staircase. As I ascended, the flashlight's beam swept over dark portraits in big gilt frames, suits of tarnished armour on the landing, and the antlered head of an elk or two. When I got to the second floor, I didn't know what to do. There were so many hallways and rooms. And what was I going to do when I found the source of the creaking? I'd done some crazy things in my life, but this was sheer lunacy. Hell, for all I knew, Rorke had friends, maybe a lot of friends.

The creaking had stopped, but when last heard it had come from somewhere down the long wood-panelled hallway that stretched out before me. So I ventured on. I had no idea where I was going and increasingly felt as if I were letting myself get sucked into a maze from which I'd never emerge. Finally I came to another staircase, this one no doubt leading to the third floor.

I couldn't hear anything, but I figured my Minotaur had to be upstairs somewhere. The hero and the villain in the movies always ended up at the top of something, didn't they? Freud and Mom wouldn't have it any other way.

When I got to the third floor, I wandered down a few more hallways until I came to a sign that indicated the stairs leading to one of the castle's two towers. Why not? I thought. I'd come this far. What were a few more stairs? Only these were the spiral metal kind, and so narrow even one person had trouble slipping up them.

I was moving much more slowly. I didn't really want to find out who or what lay in wait at the top of the stairs. But I couldn't let go. Emerging from the staircase and into the starlit sky of the open staircase was a great relief. I'd been getting claustrophobic in the mildewy confines of the castle.

In front of me the city sprawled in all its winking glory, first and foremost the concrete pylon of the CN Tower, attended, as usual, by its bank building buddies. Blotting out the base of the tower, though, was the dark outline of a man standing right up against the battlement. He had his back to me, and I had a chilly feeling that I'd been through all this before.

"It's about time, Mickey. What took you so long?"

The Boston accent with its slight mocking tone was unmistakable. So was the shaggy mane that stood out in silhouette from his head.

"Well, Jack, you never were good at directions."

He turned around. I couldn't really see his face, but I knew a grin was probably spreading slowly across those sloppy features. Jack was dressed in black— black turtleneck, black sport jacket, black loafers. He looked like a ninja gremlin in need of a haircut.

"Cool," I said, trying to smile. "The threads, I mean."

Jack didn't say anything. We stood there in the night at the top of a pseudo-Scottish castle overlooking a bright and shiny city perched on the edge of a big flat lake. There was a moon, and it hung over us, unreal in its fullness, so close all I had to do, it seemed, was reach up and grab it.

"You couldn't let it alone, could you, Mickey?" Jack whispered wearily, a certain steeliness in his voice.

"You know me, Jack. I can't stop until I know everything."

"And what do you know? What do you really know?"

"Why, Jack? Just tell me that. You had everything."

He snorted. "Does there always have to be a why? Sometimes things just are."

"There has to be a reason."

"Poor Mickey. A man in search of answers who doesn't even know the questions. You were always like that. Always needing to know without ever really knowing the need. Some investigative reporter. Do you ever wonder why you never really see the truth? It's because there isn't any. It doesn't exist. Never has. Hell, Mickey, even if there was such a thing, you'd never find it. I counted on that."

"I found you, didn't I?"

"Only because I let you."

My mind raced as I made a peripheral search for Nik Rorke. I couldn't see him, but that didn't mean much. Rorke had a talent for materializing out of thin air. My gut told me he was nearby. Slowly I moved away from the staircase, trying to think of something else to say to Jack, something to keep him talking. "Why here?" I blurted, painfully aware of the prolonged silence. "Why Casa Loma?"

He turned and faced the bright city again. "Quite a view, don't you think? Gives you the illusion you can see forever. Besides, I like this old heap. You know, the guy who built it was really something. This city never knew what to make of him. A romantic capitalist. Made a fortune from hydro, then spent millions building this crazy house. He dreamed of the Lady of the Lake and Ivanhoe in a land of Sunday blue laws and sanctimonious rectitude. He was a doer, old Hank was. At twenty, in 1879, he ran a hundred yards in twelve seconds. That held as a record until Jesse Owens beat it in 1936 at the Berlin Olympics. Pellatt built the first hydro-electric plant at Niagara Falls and made seventeen million bucks."

"You should've been a history prof, Jack. But your hero lost his shirt erecting his own personal Camelot. Worse, when it was turned over to the Kiwanis Club in the thirties, he had to pay admission like anyone else and died with a few paltry thousand to his name. You going to follow in his footsteps?"

He turned to face me. "I don't have heroes, Mickey. They're as meaningless as truth. But I do like a little theatricality, and this place has a lot of that. What's more, it fits in nicely with our plans. Guy breaks into Casa Loma to steal whatever he can find. You see, this guy's desperate. Used to be a high-priced reporter, but now he's out of work and down on his luck. Picked up a nasty drug habit, probably from a fat friend who should be dead. The cops will find a lot of drug paraphernalia in the guy's apartment. They'll find some traces of coke in his corpse. And they'll find a dead security guard who tried to stop him. But they won't find Vip. We'll make sure of that."

I didn't like his emphasis on "we." Once again I visually checked every nook and cranny in a frantic attempt to locate significant others. Keep him talking, I ordered myself. "You screwed up with Jerry, though. He's still alive."

"It doesn't really matter. Even if your friend recovers, all he knows is how good Vip is— was— with a knife."

Ask him a question. Quick. "You had everything, Jack. Brigit, Conor, a great academic career, friends, your writing—"

"Everything? You keep harping on that. What would you know? My writing? Worm pickers get paid more than I'll ever get from my poetry. And even if I got the full professorship those pompous shits in the English department will never let me have, I wouldn't come close in a lifetime of teaching to what that manuscript got me."

"Money? I thought you didn't care about it."

"We're talking two million dollars, Mickey. Two million tax free. But you're right. It's not just the money. It's what it represents. It's what I can do with it. Hell, it's not even that. It's the thrill. I've felt more alive since I got into this. The power. You don't get this kind of high spoon-feeding semi-literate undergrads."

"And the people you killed?"

"I didn't kill anybody."

"What about Sharon Praeger, Donald Yates, Garrett Macpherson, Cedric Shaw?"

"Human nature, Mickey. That's what killed them. I provided the set-up and human nature did the rest. Poor Sharon was a nympho. Just couldn't get enough until she had more than she could possibly handle. Yates? Fear ruled that snotty-nosed coward. And fear pushed him in front of that car."

"With a little help from Vip and Rorke or whoever was driving."

"Mere details. As for Shaw, it was pure greed. His kind never have enough. And then there's you. The dead should have scared you off but good."

I winced. "What about Brigit and Conor?" I asked, my mind racing.

"You tell me. C'mon, it's no secret. You've always wanted to get into my wife's panties. 'Fess up. I'm sure you'd like the whole package, Conor included.

Isn't that what scuppered your marriage? No kids? That and your big fuck-up as a reporter? You always wanted to be a family man. And you could have been. You could have been part of my family. I tried to protect you. I could have had you snuffed, but I didn't. I put my trust in your nature, maybe too much. After everything dies down, I'm going to retire, devote myself to the Muse, and build my own castle in Hawaii. And you could have come and visited, like old times, just the three of us— you, Brigit, and me. And Conor, of course. You could have written that novel you used to tell me about, the one about your parents."

"Does Brigit know about any of this? Is she in on it, too?"

"Brigit?" Jack exploded with a cross between a cackle and a guffaw. "Little innocent Brigit? Hell, no! But I knew you'd go anywhere she told you to. You'd go straight into Hell if Brigit beckoned. It's your nature, Mickey. Plain and simple."

"What did you do with Carole Rutland? What was her weakness? Trusting you?"

"Sure, why not? Carole was a screwed-up kid looking for Daddy. I guess you could say she found him."

"Macpherson?"

"That randy old goat? Hell, no! Macpherson had a yen for pretty young things, so I got Carole to apply as his assistant, then I let nature take its course."

"So when she helped you get *Cardenio,* you sicced Vip and Rorke on her. Or maybe you did it yourself."

"Now there's a mystery, Mickey, one I was hoping you really would solve. I'd love to know what happened to Carole."

"What about the videotape and all the others I saw at Shaw's hideaway?" I felt the tape inside my jacket pressing against my chest. "What's so important about the tape? Is your boss on it?"

"You should've taken a look at it. You'd find it interesting. I'm glad you didn't, though. You might have shown it to someone else, and that would've been embarrassing. You'd be amazed what's on it, but, no, my... client isn't on that tape or any others. Shaw had some pretty kinky hobbies, and I guess I got a little indiscreet in the presence of his camcorder."

"Who is your boss, Jack? A lot of people have died just so he can own some pieces of paper that may or may not be Shakespeare. Even if the manuscript is authentic, he can never tell anybody, let alone try to sell it."

"I can assure you my client doesn't need money. We all have quirks. Apparently his is the satisfaction of owning something truly unique."

Both of us heard a metallic click cut the cool night air. For a brief moment Jack's gaze flickered to the deep shadows of the entranceway to the spiral staircase.

I licked my dry lips, every muscle in me tensing. "And now what?"

"Not much choice, is there? If you hadn't kept sticking your nose into the shit... well, it's too late now."

"You can't kill me, Jack."

"I won't have to."

Nik Rorke, garbed in the usual black, stepped out of the shadows. "You really are a stupid fucker, aren't you?" Rorke's flinty eyes skewered me, and try as I might, I couldn't wrench my eyes away from him.

"Mickey, I know you and Nik are old pals. I think I'll let you get reacquainted."

"Not so fast, Jacko," Nik rasped. Mercifully he had released my eyes and was now scrutinizing Jack as if he were a particularly interesting cockroach.

Jack visibly stiffened and started to say something.

"The boss wants things real clean," Rorke said, cutting him off.

"I'm the boss, Rorke. What the hell are you trying to pull?"

"Sorry, Jacko, but you're just hired help, too. I take my orders from the same guy you do. Not so long ago he coughed up a lot of money for a little housecleaning." Rorke's lips, never more than a tight slit in his lower face, became as taut as steel high-tension wire, and the silenced pistol in his hand sounded twice, as if the air had been suddenly let out of a car's tires.

Jack's eyes popped, a tiny gasp slipped from his lips, and he slid to the stone floor. As I watched him crumple, a year seemed to pass by slowly, while another part of me screamed. The gun and flashlight in my hands hit the floor the same time as Jack's body.

The next thing I knew I was crashing down the metal spiral staircase, half tumbling to the landing below. Hardly stopping to catch my breath, convinced a bullet would hit me in the back of the skull any moment, cursing myself for dropping the gun, I stumbled and staggered down to the main floor of the mock castle. Panicky and terrified, I kept right on down to the basement. When I got there, I nearly ran over a sign indicating a tunnel leading to the mansion's stables.

There were a few muted night lights on in the basement, so I could see a bit, but the tunnel was pitch-black. I had no way of knowing what lay beyond the faint illumination, yet I lurched forward, anyway. There was no doubt what was behind me.

The tunnel was dank and cold, and when I brushed against a wall, the dampness made my flesh crawl. Rationally I knew the wall must be concrete, but in the dark it seemed alive, sentient, and its slimy exterior writhed, as if my touch had awakened it. Numb with terror, I came to a halt and started swatting my upper arms, warding off unspeakable invisible things I was convinced were dive-bombing me. Then I heard something spatter. Had it come from behind? Dripping water? Footsteps?

One fear overcame another and I plunged on into a world so black that I couldn't see my own body. In a tunnel of nameless horrors there was one that was all too real, and I was certain it was gaining on me fast.

I don't know how far I ran. The tunnel, I reasoned, couldn't be that long. A couple of times I fell, only to spring up again when my nerve endings slid over the clammy carapace of the beast whose gut I had invaded. Finally, after what seemed to be an immeasurable stretch of time, I spied a light ahead. Pressing on, I came to some stairs and, hardly hesitating, clambered up them.

I had made it! The floor beneath my feet was brick or tile. The surrounding room was spacious. I was in the stables or the carriage house. As I tried to catch my breath, I strained to pick up the sound of Nik Rorke pounding through the tunnel, but all was silent. Then I heard a crunching noise and I bolted for the broad wooden door in front of me. Clawing frantically at the old wood, I poked and prodded, pressed and pushed until the great door gave way. Almost tumbling onto the gravel path outside, I righted myself and sped across the path and adjacent lawn to the wrought-iron fence that enclosed the open area. Desperately I grabbed at the cold metal, trying to hoist myself up and over. In my panic, I was sure something was tugging at my feet. That was all I needed. With an uncharacteristic burst of energy I hurled myself over and landed in a heap on the other side. But I was far from free. I had to keep moving. There was no doubt in my mind that Rorke would shoot me dead right here as well as anywhere else.

At that moment a beaten-up black sedan pulled up to the curb, completely disorienting me. Had Rorke simply climbed into his car and driven round to cut me off?

"Mickey?" a voice growled from the car.

It was Frank Kaplan. This news took me a moment to digest, then I flung myself at his car door. As soon as I climbed in, I yelled, "Quick! Step on it! He'll start shooting any moment."

"Who?"

"Rorke. Nik Rorke. He's right behind me."

"No one was chasing you, Mickey. I saw you come out of the stables like a bat out of hell, but nobody was behind you."

"But... what are you doing here? Don't get me wrong. I'm overjoyed that you are. But you couldn't have known I'd be here."

"They told me at the division that someone had called. When we found Cedric Shaw's body, I knew something was up. We were beating the woods for Rorke and his playmate Vip, figuring they were probably at the bottom of Shaw's murder. We got a call about gunshots up here at Casa Loma. We found Vip and a dead security guard. I took a spin up here on a wild hunch."

"Did you find Rorke?" I almost shouted.

"No such luck. They're checking the grounds now, and there's another couple of units on the way."

"Tell them to look in the open tower. They'll find another corpse."

"Whose?"

"Someone I thought I knew."

STATION XIV

Funny how you think you can sleep for a week and then you can't. A few days had passed since that terrifying night at Casa Loma, and I hadn't gotten much shut-eye. When I gave my statement at Kaplan's division, I'd also handed over the videotape, but later, after I asked, he gave me a copy of it.

I wish he hadn't. I keep playing it over and over. The first thing I'd done after getting the tape was to rent a VCR. Now, in my living room, I'm watching it for the— shit, I don't know how many times. All that time looking for Carole, and there she is on the TV screen. And I mean all of her. She's peeling off her clothes, piece by piece, doing a striptease for someone off-camera, someone who keeps telling her, "Do it, baby! Do it!"

Carole's not very happy as she sways to what sounds like something low and sweet from Charlie Parker's sax. Maybe "Loverman."

"Do it!" the voice insists. "Do it for Daddy!" And the voice is unmistakably Jack Malone's.

The cops were overjoyed. They'd pinned the whole mess on Jack and wrapped it up with a bow. But what did they really know? Rorke? He'd vanished into the night as he always did. He hadn't killed me, and that wasn't like Nik. Loose ends were bad for business.

I suppose Jerry was another loose end for Rorke. He had snapped out of the coma, and the doctors said he'd make a full recovery. Like me, Jerry didn't know anything about Rorke's boss. As for Nik himself, maybe he didn't care if Jerry or I could finger him. Still, I knew I'd be watching my back for a long time to come.

The rich guy who'd set everything in motion? We'd never know who he was. *Cardenio*? Was it real? Did it even exist? Was it the straight goods? No one cared. Maybe even the old geezer who'd paid two million for it didn't, either. I could see him, in a giant vault somewhere, maybe in Switzerland, sitting in his very own plush red velvet chair, watching his private acting company bring to life a Shakespearean play that no one else would ever see. I could almost see the twisted smile on the bastard's face.

And what about Carole? Who gave a damn about her? The old lady on the phone who'd gotten me curious in the first place and who might have been her mother? The cops had half-heartedly tried to locate Carole's parents and come up empty. Surely a mother knows where her daughter is.

Jack had said he didn't have a clue about Carole's whereabouts. If he didn't know, who did? Hammer Harry? Herbert Sutcliffe? Or had she taken a powder, knowing full well how she might end up? That's what the cops figured. They had enough stiffs on their hands. Or had someone else killed her? Someone no one would ever suspect? But I didn't want to pursue that line of thought.

My gaze flickers across the screen. Carole is down to her bra and panties. She's a thin woman, tall but bony. I can see her ribs. Her hips move slowly to the music. She doesn't look any happier, but her tongue darts between her teeth like a serpent's, and she wets her lips suggestively.

"Do it!" Jack croaks. "Do it, baby!"

Carole moves closer to the camera, one finger inching under her plain white left bra cup. I can see a thin film of sweat on her face, but it's her eyes I want to peer into, hoping to find some answers. But, even though I try hard not to, I glance downward as the bra loosens and releases two pert little breasts with enormous nipples, the left one with a tiny tattoo on the areola. I squeeze my eyes, but I can't make out what it is.

"C'mon, baby, all the way!" exhorts Jack, mounting excitement in his Boston accent.

For a second I almost think I spot panic, maybe fear, in Carole's off-centre green eyes, but maybe that's because I want to. Then her long fingers slide down her pale belly to her lacy white panties, playing with the elastic, snapping it teasingly, briefly giving a flash of tawny pubic hair. I can almost hear Billie Holiday singing,

> The night is cold and I'm so all alone.
> I'd give my soul just to call you my own.
> Loverman, oh, where can you be?

I hunch over on my orange wreck of a chesterfield. The sweat drips while my eyes weld themselves to the screen. The hardness grows, and I shift uncomfortably.

"Do it! Do it! Do it!" Jack crows.

And she does. The panties slip down her long, spidery legs, and she steps out of them, totally nude, and a little self-conscious.

There is a moment of stillness, and then she widens her legs to the last sinewy chords of Parker's "Loverman." A disembodied finger suddenly juts into the picture and parts the lips of Carole's vulva. The camera is tight on her midsection now. I can't see her face, but I can hear her moaning softly.

And then briefly, very briefly, a head fills the screen and attaches itself to Carole's crotch. The camera shows Jack's tongue thrusting into Carole's creamy cunt as he mutters, "Come to Daddy, baby. Come to Daddy." Then the TV explodes in electronic snow, and it's over.

There's more on the tape. Other encounters between Carole and Jack, some with various people visible— Cedric Shaw, Sharon Praeger, Donald Yates. No wonder Jack wanted the tape. It connected him with too many corpses.

But what of Carole? As I stare into the TV snow, I think about Brigit. She's on her way to Switzerland already. She stuck around long enough for Jack's funeral. There weren't too many people at that affair, despite all the friends Jack had. The media had a field day with the story of Jack the Monster. They're still engaged in a frenzy. Jack even pushed Hammer Harry off the front pages.

Brigit didn't say goodbye. It was as if she'd been prepared to go for some time. She's headed for Zurich where, apparently, she plans to study at the Jung Institute. Conor is with her. I never got the chance to ask her about Carole. Maybe I didn't really want to.

Perhaps if the billionaire who snatched *Cardenio* is in Switzerland somewhere, Brigit will run into him. She'd make a pretty good Luscinda. I keep getting impulses to go to Switzerland. But I won't, for my own sake. The cops keep looking for that two million of Jack's. I don't think they'll ever find it.

In a little while, I'm going to visit Jerry in the hospital. We've got a lot of catching up to do. He wants me to bring him a bottle of single-malt Scotch, a couple of cigars, and some chocolate mints. He says he's taken up smoking in the hospital. Just like Jerry.

The chill of winter is in the air. It's going to be a tough one to get through, yet, strangely, I feel I will. I suppose I did solve something, after all: myself. At least a little bit.